THE
LIGHTHOUSE CAFÉ
AND RETREAT

A MYSTICAL ADVENTURE

PAULETTE BLOMELEY

BALBOA.PRESS

A DIVISION OF HAY HOUSE

Balboa Press books may be ordered through booksellers or by contacting:

Balboa Press
A Division of Hay House
1663 Liberty Drive
Bloomington, IN 47403
www.balboapress.com.au
AU TFN: 1 800 844 925 (Toll Free inside Australia)
AU Local: 0283 107 086 (+61 2 8310 7086 from outside Australia)

Because of the dynamic nature of the Internet, any web addresses or links contained in this book may have changed since publication and may no longer be valid. The views expressed in this work are solely those of the author and do not necessarily reflect the views of the publisher, and the publisher hereby disclaims any responsibility for them.

The author of this book does not dispense medical advice or prescribe the use of any technique as a form of treatment for physical, emotional, or medical problems without the advice of a physician, either directly or indirectly. The intent of the author is only to offer information of a general nature to help you in your quest for emotional and spiritual well-being. In the event you use any of the information in this book for yourself, which is your constitutional right, the author and the publisher assume no responsibility for your actions.

Any people depicted in stock imagery provided by Getty Images are models, and such images are being used for illustrative purposes only. Certain stock imagery © Getty Images.

Print information available on the last page.

ISBN: 978-1-5043-2209-6 (sc)
ISBN: 978-1-5043-2229-4 (e)

Balboa Press rev. date: 08/27/2020

CHAPTER 1

Grace had a long day tying up the formalities for her grand purchase. The last few months of deliberating whether to go through with it or not had exhausted her.

A part of her was so excited, but the mental and emotional exhaustion had taken its toll on her, the weariness that anxiety had created within her was overpowering.

She would have to celebrate once she'd had a good night's sleep, it had been a long time, there had been so much planning to do.

She had made her final decision, one that still made her heartbeat fast just at the thought of it; well it was done now, she had bought the old Guest House on the cliff's edge, on the outskirts of a lovely little town named Sea Cliff.

She felt pure joy and minor trepidation battling within her.

After all this was not a practical move for Grace, but she knew it was a decision made from her heart and now she would do a lot of praying that all would turn out the way she visualised, her plans were realistic—at least she hoped so.

Just one week and she would have the keys in her hands, it all felt so surreal, if it wasn't for an uncle in Scotland she never would have been able to buy the Guest House which, after many weeks of pondering, she had decided to call The Lighthouse Retreat and Cafe.

She would sell books, crystals, some local artwork as well as have a small cafe, she would make it warm and cosy, the weather got very cold on the coast of Victoria.

The icy chill of the winds coming from the ocean could render you numb.

There were ten rooms in the Guest House that she could use, the other ten would need a lot of refurbishing before she could accommodate them, but that suited her fine, that would be all she could manage to look after until she had the means to employ others.

She had no family, her parents passed away in an accident when she was five years old, she was brought up by her beautiful Auntie Yvonne; her heart swelled with love when she thought of her loving kind aunty, who had brought her up and taught her such fine morals, the day she died had left a mighty chasm in Grace's chest.

Not a day passed without her feeling Yvonne's Spirit around her and this gave her a form of peace, although the physical loss was great. Her Aunty was a wise lady indeed, she had chosen to stay single after the premature death of her beloved Joe.

Joe was a seaman, he drowned in a horrendous storm, the ship sunk and all on it died. Aunty said that was the way he would have wanted to have gone, he always knew the sea would claim him one day, he believed that was his destiny!

There was an old light house situated beside the Guest House, Grace was unsure what she would do with that, but she had an idea of having Astronomy and Astrology retreats and once the old stairs were fixed guests could go and Star Gaze from the top platform.

Then there was the main house which was an old red brick homestead, it boasted seven very small rooms, eloquently decked out with antique furnishings. It had four fire places, one in the main dining room, one in the lounge room, one in the main bedroom and one in a large room she would make her office.

So many ideas running around in Grace's head, she would write them all down and then work through them one at a time. Otherwise she was overwhelming herself with the possibilities, she had to pinch herself she felt as if she was living a dream within a dream.

Well the time had arrived, it was sad to say goodbye to the little cottage that her and her Aunty had lived in for the past thirty-five years. There were many times when Grace had travelled and lived in other parts of the country, and some short stints overseas.

She loved coming back to the coastline that she would always call her home. Yvonne would have been so proud to see Grace turning the key to her new life.

Never in Grace's wildest dreams would she have envisioned that one day it would belong to her. It was a place that her and her Aunty had stayed in many times, because they both loved the old Guest House; it had such a powerful aura of memories and made one feel Nostalgic; for what one was not even sure of, maybe a time of innocence and less complications, or just maybe we always looked back to the past through romantic eyes, not at the harsh truths that it held.

Grace wondered why humans always seemed to think that other times were better than now, whether it be the past or the future, she pondered that they were not really better or worse just different, that's all.

As she stepped in through the doorway the dank, musky odours flooded her senses, wow, she thought, this place needs some serious airing out, luckily it was sunny outside.

The electric heater she was mighty grateful for, because she had not even thought of ordering the wood with so many other chores occupying her mind.

She walked over to the beautiful carved mirror, which to her knowledge had come from the East. She loved the intricacies of its carvings.

She could only imagine how long someone must have put into it. It had birds and flowers carved all around it with beautiful patterns interweaving through all of it, yes, it was a grand masterpiece and Grace would treasure it always.

Whilst taking in every single detail Grace caught a glimpse of her reflection, she looked closer and felt somewhat surprised at her appearance, she had changed of that there was no doubt.

She had deep blue eyes that slanted down at the corners, giving the sad dog effect.

Her hair was light brown and tended to get sun streaked when she was in the sun and surf a lot.

It was ringlets hanging past her shoulders, it was hard to manage so she wore it up most of the time.

She had rather full lips and her mouth quite small as was her nose. She had noticed wrinkles appearing around her eyes.

Her skin had a light scattering of freckles, but she did still manage to get quite tanned when she wanted.

She was no great beauty but very attractive in a unique style. Grace was 165cm tall, an average height and quite a slim build. She had made peace with her looks at a young age, she knew there was no point in comparing herself to others; there was no competition after all.

She made a point of not getting sucked into the whole superficial beauty aspect that affected many girls, giving themselves unrealistic goals. Too much media influence could make one feel that way.

When she finished studying her somewhat altered appearance, she noted that she was more mature looking and even with all the pressure she had been under, she looked more peaceful.

Yes, she was indeed pleased with the confident woman she was becoming. She saw a wisdom in herself she had never noticed before and she liked it—a lot.

She realised she had to take notes of all the jobs that needed to be addressed before the opening, for she would go crazy if she tried to keep it all in her mind.

She reached for the pen and paper in her bag and went completely still when she felt tingles going through the top of her head and then running down her back and through her legs, when it stopped Grace was stunned never had she felt anything as beautiful and powerful as that, whatever it was she thought, thank you, thank you for being with me.

She was not sure what or whom she was thanking, but she knew that was a sensation she had not experienced before, not that powerful anyway, she had felt slight tingling from her parents and her aunt but nothing remotely as powerful as what she had just experienced.

She sat on the dusty old lounge, her legs felt too weak to support her weight, she wasn't sure whether to laugh or cry, she was a little rattled by the experience.

And then they came in a mighty flood; all the pent up tears from the last three months, where her daily moods were oscillating between excitement, fear, guilt, so many different emotions she had been experiencing.

She wished she had of had someone to guide her, but as things turned out the money had been bequeathed after the death of her Aunt, so she was alone in her decisions and what to do with the large sum of money that she had acquired.

How ironic it was that all her loved ones that passed away didn't have much to leave her, neither did she want their money, their love was all she ever wanted there was not a materialistic bone in Grace Bliss's body.

When she did have money left to her it was from an Uncle on her mother's side of the family, he had only met Grace for a few days when she was travelling through Scotland, she stayed with him; she had no idea he had felt any affection for her, although they did get along really well, she was completely overwhelmed when she had learned of her rather large inheritance, the saddest thing was she had no loved ones to share it with.

So that is why she decided on the old Guest House, she wanted to turn it into somewhere affordable for the travellers on a tight budget, some would have the option to work for their food and accommodation, she desperately wanted to create a harmonious atmosphere where all that stayed there felt comfortable and safe.

She also wanted travellers of all ages; not just young backpackers, although they most certainly would be welcome once she had the rooms sorted out. She would focus on the cafe, that part really excited her, it was going to be completely vegetarian, she would grow as much of her own produce as she possibly could.

CHAPTER 2

Grace woke in the middle of the night, she could hear a slight humming sound but had no idea where it was coming from, she got out of her bed in total resistance as the cold latched on to her, she had no idea why she got up, but the humming noise had her curious, silly fool she thought, should have stayed in the warm bed.

She opened the curtains and looked outside toward the ocean, there was a full moon shining down on the water, the sight before her was a fine vision indeed, the moon had a rainbow ring around it that reflected on to the ocean's surface, Grace was completely entranced by what she was looking at, words have no place in something as beautiful as this scene before me, thought Grace.

The humming was getting louder, Grace was starting to feel fear until a huge surge of love engulfed her, it warmed every molecule of her being.

Grace was completely transfixed at her window, until she heard the word "Greetings," come from behind her, she turned without time to think, and there stood the most lovely, handsome male specimen Grace had ever laid eyes on.

"Who are you, and what are you doing in my room?"

"I am sorry to alarm you, I just thought it is time I revealed myself to you, after all you were the one were you not, that made the wish on your fortieth birthday to meet your twin flame.

You wished it with your whole heart, it reverberated out into the Universe, how could I possibly have refused your call, when you said it so authentically, so adamantly!"

Grace stared with her mouth open, "how could I have asked for you?

I asked for my twin flame, just like all the other people at the seminar that were there to meet theirs, it just so happened to coincide with my fortieth birthday.

You must excuse me but I didn't ask for a mirage, I wanted the real thing, although you are a sight indeed, in fact I think such masculine beauty belongs to a fairy tale."

"You think I am not real, that I speak these words for the joy of it, I am sorry to disappoint you Grace, but you see I am truly your twin flame; as you humans put it, I am sorry I do not have the physicality that you do.

You and I have had many times apart and many times together on this planet, this way we learn more and the knowledge and lessons we learn become both of us because together we are one."

Grace looked and listened, "I don't want to believe a word you're saying.

"Trust your heart Grace, what other point of truth do you have?"

"So then, do you have a name?" "Forgive me, my name is Sorin."

Sorin reached his hand out toward Grace, Grace just looked at it, thinking what a strange dream she was having, well nothing to lose she thought as she touched his hand, Grace jerked back, the energy transference nearly knocked her over.

Grace started crying and then she let go completely and sobbed and sobbed, Sorin watched with all of his love reaching out to Grace, he remembered what it was like to be human, he remembered the intensity of the emotions, sometimes they were so overwhelming you didn't feel like you would survive them, like a raging sea in the storm, tumultuous and dangerous they could override logic if you didn't get a hold of them.

Once Grace had released all her pain, she quietly said, "I didn't want you, I wanted a man to share my life with!"

Sorin looked at Grace with sadness, "I understand, that you need company, you should have wished for a partner not a twin flame" Grace looked at Sorin and said "well now I really understand the saying be careful what you wish for, I put everything into that wish, and here you are."

"Well Sorin, where have you come from?"

"I come from the same planet as you do, it's in a higher dimensional vibration, it is where our soul family resides, it could be called Istara. In the higher vibrational dimensions and planets we have no real need for names, all is recognised by ones energy pattern, all forms of Consciousness are unique no matter what their appearance at the time, for all is in a constant state of flux but always unique.

As humans you have forgotten all of this knowledge consciously so you can experience what you are here to learn, for if you remembered all that you are, that would be very confusing to you.

Alas it is time for humans to wake up to their cosmic consciousness, it exists in every one of you.

The cosmic cells of your brain and DNA are now being awakened and stimulated.

It is essential that you know yourself first and to do this you must go within and connect with the vital essence of all life; whilst being consciously connected to this divine essence you have the ability to discover all you could possibly imagine and a lot more!

I have said enough for now, I think you need time to integrate all I have said, and by the way Grace, it is indeed true that you have free will, so if you do not wish to see me again that shall be so, I will leave it with you.

I have something for you," Sorin handed Grace a beautiful clear quartz crystal. If you wish to contact me just sit silently and think of me whilst you hold the crystal. When you feel it vibrate intensely you will know I am aware of your contact."

"You are right Sorin, I need time to sort through my feelings on all of this, I thank you for all you have shared with me, but in all honesty I am not sure whether I will be in contact or not, if not, I am sorry if I have disappointed you"

"You have not disappointed me Grace, I am learning in many dimensions and on many planets at the moment, so this is not imperative to my growth, we will be together again no matter what, when and where is not important for there is no time or space where the true Spirit resides, we all are multi-dimensional beings living many realities simultaneously."

A part of Grace wanted to yell out, please don't go as Sorin started fading away, but nothing would come out of her mouth, she felt a sadness in her heart when he was gone.

Oh no, was all she could think, what am I going to do?

She went to bed climbed under the doona, curled up into the foetal position and fell fast asleep.

When Grace woke up she recalled having a strange dream about a handsome man with white curly hair and the most stunning blue eyes she had ever seen, they were a clear sky blue. She could not believe how vivid the dream had been.

She started thinking about her day ahead and realised she was holding something with a sharp edge, she looked into her hand to see a lovely quartz crystal with tiny little rainbows shining in it.

Oh no, it cannot be, this cannot be real. She felt anger and sadness and then just shock, it was all real, the lovely man named Sorin was real, at least she knew she did not have to see him again what a relief that was to her.

The words he said to her touched her so deeply, they affected her in a way that no others in her life had, she knew to stay sane she would have to put it all to the back of her mind, because she had so much work to do.

Her days passed by in a haze of phone calls, appointments, builders, plumbers, electricians, she was a little over it all, but stopping or even prolonging was a luxury she could not afford, the sooner she had the place up and running the better.

Today she was going to spend the day on Ebay seeing if she could buy the linen she required, if not she would have to make a trip to the city, something she was trying to avoid at all costs. She was a bit vague to be driving around in the city, with so much going on, so much to remember.

Not to mention the beautiful face that kept popping into her mind, she had no idea what to do about that, part of her would have so loved to talk to Sorin, but the human part said, "don't go there you will take on more that you can handle."

At this stage that felt like the voice she should listen to, if only she had someone she could talk to about it all, it made her feel even more alone that she couldn't share all she was going through.

Grace realised it was time she had some company, the big place felt so lonely on her own, most of the rooms were ready, she just needed some help with the final touches.

She had some gardening to do, and some old pieces of furniture that needed sanding back and staining, she loved the feeling of accomplishment after finishing such tasks, it was just the time to do it she lacked at the moment.

So she bit the bullet and put an ad on the Internet, she hoped for a couple to stay, she would like the company and she really didn't need the distraction of single men around her.

Since she turned forty she felt like the dating part of her life had come to a complete standstill, there were so many other things in her life now that would require all of her attention, she just hoped she wasn't using the Guest House as an excuse not to have intimacy – how easy that would be after all she had been through; losing all her loved ones, she wasn't sure if she would ever open her heart to anyone again, at least not intimately anyway, she decided now it was time to have an open mind and heart learning to love everyone unconditionally, she wanted to work hard at not having any judgement in her, she hoped to attract people from all walks of life, after all that's what life was about; learning and sharing.

At least she knew not to search for her twin flame now, that would make things simpler for her.

She felt like ringing the lovely lady who conducted the 'Find Your Twin Flame' seminar and tell her another version of Twin Flames, that thought put a smile on her face.

The first people to answer her add were three young people travelling around Australia, they were on the West Coast and taking their time heading to the East.

Grace had a good feeling about them, there were two girls and a guy, she had said yes without meeting them, she had gained an uncannily accurate intuition since her little meeting with Sorin, her mind felt so clear and sharp.

She hadn't picked up the crystal since the morning after, she was afraid if she touched it it would call him in and she was not sure whether she would ever do it.

Sometimes she had almost done it out of loneliness, but berated herself for even thinking of it. She was still sceptical about many aspects of it, but one thing she could not deny was that he was standing in front of her talking to her, if he had not left the crystal then she would have been able to deny the whole scenario to herself, but that was not to be; for better or worse.

She had a feeling she had been dreaming of Sorin every night, but couldn't remember anything with any real clarity, just snippets of conversations and pictures not enough to put together to make any sense.

Grace got out of bed feeling excited about the prospect of meeting her first visitors. Depending on how things went Grace was hoping they would stay for at least a month, that was how long she gave herself to be ready to open. It all depended on how motivated the young people were and how hard they were prepared to work for their keep.

Grace casually walked outside when she heard the car pull up, she felt silly that her heart was beating fast with anticipation, part of her was yelling, "oh no, what have I done inviting three total strangers to stay," too late to pull out now.

She was nicely surprised to see the first girl come toward her, she looked at least in her thirties.

"Hi I'm Sarah," she said with her hand outstretched toward Grace, Grace took her hand and said "Hi Sarah pleased to meet you I'm Grace"

Sarah had a lovely warm smile that made Grace feel immediately at Peace.

Grace looked in awe at the stunning girl walking toward her with wild blue black hair, piercings and some tattoo's.

Grace felt an amazing Aura about the Girl/Woman.

Grace extended her hand this time and said, "Hi I'm Grace, nice to meet you." Grace felt a slight jolt when she touched the girl's hand.

"Hi Grace, I'm Salome, nice to meet you."

The two girls looked in each other's eyes for what seemed an eternity. Grace had such a powerful feeling she knew the girl from somewhere.

Salome yelled out, "hurry up Damon what are you doing?" "I'm coming," Damon replied.

Grace looked to see a most handsome man coming her way. He had dark hair and olive skin.

"Grace this is Damon, my partner."

"Good to meet you Grace." "And you Damon," replied Grace. They looked deeply into each other's eyes and once again there was that recognition that Grace had felt with Salome.

Damon said, "Wow, this place is awesome, thanks for inviting us, can we have a bit of a look around before we get settled?" "Absolutely!" said Grace, 'take your time, I was just about to make some lunch, it should be ready in about half an hour. Take your time, just don't go up the stairs of the light house, I will be getting them fixed as soon as I can get a builder that has time."

"I'll have a look for you" said Damon enthusiastically, "I have done a lot of that sort of thing lately."

"That would be fantastic," said Grace feeling very impressed.

Grace found out over lunch that Damon and Salome had been travelling around Australia for twelve months, and that there was a purpose for their journey that they would fill Grace in on when they had more time. Right now they were full of excitement for their present circumstances, they had been lead here by higher forces at that they had no doubt, now they would find out why.

There was something really familiar about them both, but Grace could not quite put her finger on what it was. She felt confident that all would be revealed in its own time.

Grace had no worries about them working, Damon was already outside cutting wood for the fires. Salome and Sarah were putting the final touches to the rooms that Grace wanted to start renting out.

Grace made them a beautiful vegetarian lasagne for dinner, they sat around the fire and told stories, of their travels.

Grace found out that Damon had been in the army in Afghanistan until he was injured.

Salome was a hairdresser and a whiz in the kitchen.

Grace could not believe her luck, how had she been so fortunate? Salome was more than willing to help get the cafe going and stay on for a while if it took off.

When Grace went to bed she had to pinch herself, she had struck gold with Salome and Damon, Sarah seemed a bit distant, she hadn't been with them for long.

She said she would be going soon she felt she was being called elsewhere.

Grace didn't mind for she knew it was Salome and Damon she had a special connection with, what she was not sure, but she was confident if she was patient she would more than likely find out.

Grace was sitting on her favourite seat, which just happened to give the most spectacular panoramic view of the coastline. The ocean was rough today, the waves were pounding against the cliff's edge.

Grace closed her eyes and let the sound lull her into a deep space of relaxation, the repetition of the waves crashing always managed to take Grace into a deep meditation, she had paid a lot of money over the years to learn different techniques of meditation, but nothing took her as deep as the rhythmic beat of the ocean.

Surrendering herself to that deep place of total peace where all was still and quiet, this was her centre this deep place had been her survival to all the great losses she had endured in her forty years of life.

This was the place where all dreams were born, and all aspects of oneself could be discovered.

This was the place that held all the answers and all the keys to the doorways that were yet to be discovered. Grace had no idea how long she had been in this space for, she had no recollection of anything except peace, but judging by the position of the sun she had been there for hours.

How strange she thought usually she had some conscious awareness of something happening, but she was completely blank. She had achieved what she was looking for, the peace to keep the strength to follow through with her plans, because sometimes she felt overwhelmed and didn't think she had the strength to go through with it all, she had seriously wondered whether she had taken on too much.

Salome and Damon had taken Sarah to Melbourne, that was where she felt her journey called her, she was very artistic and talented and there would be a lot more opportunities for her there.

Grace was happy to have a couple of nights to herself, she needed it. The stillness seemed to be calling her. She sat and meditated every chance she got, she felt it was healing her of all her past pain. She had never realised before but she actually carried guilt about being happy. Because all of her loved ones had gone, something in her felt she should live in grief.

My how complex us humans have become, the mind is a great trickster indeed, it plays all sorts of games to set off the emotions and confusion.

Mastering her mind was something Grace took very seriously. She had no intentions of letting her thoughts or her emotions control her and the only way to achieve that was to live in the absolute now. That is where the source of all life is connected, only ever in the infinite now and thoughts and emotions pull you out of that all-powerful beautiful place.

If you think about it, what is the sense of living in a past that is just that 'past', and the future not set in stone, many probable futures, depending how present we are in each moment and how consciously we create our reality.

Grace loved pondering over these things, much she had discovered by life's experiences, her mind and emotions use to be all over the place, it took a lot of work for her to find her true centre and constant practice to keep the connection.

As Grace laid in her bed she couldn't get the picture of Sorin out of her mind, and her heart longed to see him, maybe she could just call him one more time.

Grace held the crystal in her hand and took a deep breath, she felt herself relaxing immediately, she focused on Sorin's face, nothing, the crystal was lovely but she felt nothing unusual happening.

She started to think how foolish she was to believe it could be possible, she went to lay it on her bedside table and she felt it tremor gently, she thought she was imagining it, she looked at it and saw it shaking heavily now on her sweating palm, her heart started to beat fast, oh no, I have changed my mind, please don't come, but it was too late she heard the deep humming sound and then he appeared right in front of her, looking at her inquisitively.

"Greetings Grace, I am sorry but you changed your mind too late, we had already come through the time transference portal." "We? Who is we?" asked Grace bluntly, "and what time transference portal? Oh, forget I asked, I don't think I really want the answers, I am not even sure why I called you, loneliness I guess."

"May I speak Grace?" "Of course, go ahead."

Grace looked at Sorin standing in front of the window, the moonlight was shining through, he looked so lovely, so mysterious, after a while she didn't know what was shining brighter him or the moon.

He had the appearance of a physical body except it was more fluid, his movements were like a dance and his words like a song. Grace was becoming entranced by his ethereal beauty, when he said, "I would like to explain who I was talking about when I said we. You are familiar with the humming sound you hear before I appear to you" "Yes, yes I am aware of that sound"

"Come take a look out of the window"

Grace reluctantly got out of bed and walked toward the window, he held out his hand and she took it, she had never felt anything quite like it, it was so soft and yet the power emanating out of it into her hand was palpable, it was flowing like waves through her body she had never experienced anything more lovely, she wanted the feeling to last forever.

"Grace, are you alright?" "Oh sure, just feeling a little light headed." Sorin laughed, "to say the least."

Look here out the window Grace, Grace did, "do you see the light just above the lighthouse" Grace looked, "oh sure I've seen that there many times," "no take a closer look, Grace looked more intensely and she couldn't believe what she could see, it was blue light that looked to be pulsating.

"What is it?"

"Well some call it a space craft, we use it for travel, when there are a number of us going together, we do many experiments, we check your oceans and forests to see how far the damage of your chemicals and your negative energies are doing. It's not good I am afraid."

Grace looked out speechless, why was this happening to her, the worst thing was it felt right, so right, she had never really fit in anywhere except with her lovely aunty and now here was this unusual encounter occurring and nothing had ever felt so real and true in her life.

"Why? Why are you making me remember all of this, I was doing fine in my state of amnesia."

"I know you will find this hard to believe but you did choose to wake up and remember in this incarnation. Most humans are protected by forgetting, because they would literally go crazy if they remembered...now the planet is at a crucial stage of transformation, it is time for all to remember. Once one wakes up and remembers one can only hold love and respect for the completely unique and remarkable planet Earth.

But you Grace you are ready for you chose to awaken in the human state, that is why you chose the harsh family circumstances you did, because you would need all the strength and detachment that you have gained to be able to deal with what you will be experiencing and learning from now on, you won't be learning anything new, just being reminded of what you once knew and loved.

Grace could feel her heart swelling with love, she knew there were beings on that craft that she loved so very much, she just knew it!

"You will meet them in time, they are your family after all."
"So what happens now?"

"Hold my hand again and I will show you."

Grace held out her hand and next thing she knew she was flying over the ocean with Sorin, she felt so exhilarated, with a sense of freedom she could hardly fathom.

Grace was totally bewildered by the absolute happiness she felt at remembering who she really was, an infinite being, a tiny but unique part of a much vaster Universe than man could possibly conceive. At the moment she was experiencing one small aspect of her true self and it was totally mind blowing in the best way possible.

Grace's eyes could hardly take in the beauty of the stars as they were approaching them, it felt as if they were flying without any effort what so ever, she noticed that there was one star shining brighter than all of the others, the colours glowing and pulsating around it held Grace's attention without effort, there was a feeling of familiarity growing within her, Sorin looked at her for the first time since they had left, never had he looked so beautiful to Grace, she was mesmerised by him.

She started to remember many times she had shared with him. Sorin had to shut Grace's memory off for a while so she was not overwhelmed by it all, he would allow just a small fraction of her memories at a time, there were more than she could possibly integrate at this stage.

As they reached the glowing star Grace could see the surface of the star, it was a sight to behold, there were crystal palaces everywhere, as they landed outside one, Grace walked or more accurately glided toward it and put her hand out to touch the smooth surface but as she did this her hand to her surprise went straight through, it felt like some sort of liquid soft and smooth but not wet.

Grace felt like a child she looked around at the absolute beauty, it was divine creation uninterrupted, there were no dense energies to tarnish the light, it was pure and all- powerful.

Grace just wanted to look and absorb it all, some deep part of her was in a state of recognition, she felt a wisdom and knowing in her open up like a beautiful flower.

Sorin said "Grace come with me, I want to take you somewhere." Grace held out her hand to Sorin, next thing she knew she was standing in a huge dome shaped room, full of the most exotic unique flowers Grace had laid eyes on, they were being watered by colourful faeries and various forms of Nature Spirits.

Grace started giggling she couldn't help herself the faeries presence was just pure joy and love, they love every single cell of every plant. As Grace looked closer and saw there was a waterfall running at the edge of the room, her human sight couldn't accept what they were seeing, but her intuition knew it was all perfectly natural.

Grace turned toward Sorin and he had gone, all had gone strangely quiet, not one sound, even the Nature Spirits seemed to be in anticipation, something drew her toward the water and then she knew what was happening. The man had the most beautiful essence, he was so serene, talking to the faeries, Grace sensed that all in his wake were totally humbled by his presence. They looked at each other and Grace was immobilised, she knew this man with all of her heart, the only word to come out of her mouth was, 'Father'.

He smiled and nodded, it was a strange sensation as Grace felt tears even though she was not in her body.

"Aurelias?" "Yes my daughter, how pleased I am to see you again, my beloved Auraya, welcome home to Istara."

They embraced in the light and the next thing Grace knew she was lying on a crystal bed that was constantly changing colours, with Aurelias standing over her generating a beautiful luminescent green light to her, she could feel it going right through her, it was the most peaceful loving vibration, she knew it was healing something deep in her being.

She had no idea how long she was with Aurelias, it wasn't in Earth time, so there was no way of measuring it. One thing she was sure of was that he was her father in a deeply Spiritual dimension and had always been there for her on some level, if they were not together in a physical sense.

Basking in his love had given her a sense of wholeness she had not experienced before.

CHAPTER 3

After Grace's return from Istara, it took her some time to readjust to her present life. It was the perfect time for her to create her herb garden, she felt the need to get her hands into the Earth to ground and balance herself.

The journey changed the way she looked at her life. The beings were much more highly evolved than humans and yet much more humble and appreciative of all forms of life no matter what its appearance; for they knew without any doubt that all forms of consciousness are created equally and are infinite and eternal but will experience many different forms in many different dimensions and Universes, because all life is an aspect of the one creator!

As Grace was digging her garden, she heard footsteps approaching her from behind. She hadn't been expecting anyone so was very relieved to see Salome's lovely smiling face.

"Hi Grace, nice to see you."

"Yes nice to see you too Salome, did Sarah find somewhere to live?"

"We weren't sure, but we did leave her with friends, I don't think she knows what she's doing, but that's fine. I remember travelling on my Harley not knowing where I was going next. It's good for the soul to experience such freedom."

"Yes indeed, said Grace, you are right about that." "What about you Grace, how are you doing?

You look as if you have been on a journey yourself." "Well I guess you could say that Salome, I didn't think it would be that obvious."

"Well I guess that depends on who you are talking to, I have been on many journeys; not all of them physical"

Grace looked at Salome inquisitively, what was Salome trying to say, could she know? It's not possible surely!

Grace changed the subject she wasn't ready to go there with someone right now, she would get to know Salome a little first before she opened up about her inner world.

But Grace had a good intuition for a person's character and she knew she could trust Salome.

"Where is Damon?" asked Grace.

"Oh, he is getting all the timber out of the van so he can repair those stairs in the lighthouse, he loves the challenge." "Thank you so much, you don't know how much that means to me."

"I think we do, that's why we want to help. You know, we can see the vision you have for this place and we would love to do what we can to help it all come to fruition for you." Grace felt the tears slide down her cheeks, she could feel the sincerity of Salome's words, they went straight to her heart, the girls embraced both feeling a lovely authentic connection with the other.

Grace knew she was blessed to have Salome and Damon, not only were they working hard, they were loving what they were doing.

When Grace went down for dinner, she was moved to see the open fire going and the beautiful old oak table set for dinner with candles and the real silverware that Grace had found on the Internet. It had come from France and was beautifully designed, she would have loved to have known its history, unfortunately it had come from a deceased estate.

Salome walked in smiling, "well, I hope you don't mind me trying out some new recipes on you? I thought they might go well in the cafe if you like them."

"Sounds great Salome, I can't believe how much you and Damon are doing, it overwhelms me."

"Well we feel like we have struck good fortune also, we are both getting to do what we love and even be creative. I don't think you realise how wonderful this is for us, we know we are not here by coincidence Grace, we don't even believe there is such a thing. We were led here Grace for you and for us and tonight let's celebrate together and give thanks for all of our blessings."

"Absolutely, I never could have dreamed things could have turned out so well."

They ate their dinner sharing stories of their lives, with each other. Grace felt so relaxed with them both she could hardly believe her luck.

Salome had a dry wit and had Damon and Grace in stitches with her outlook on certain things, she was very intelligent noted Grace as well as gorgeous with her water blue eyes alabaster skin and blue/black hair. Damon was a lucky man. The only time Salome got serious was when she spoke of her two best friends and their partners, apparently they had all met on Magnetic Island in North Queensland, some great event had brought them together which Salome was obviously not yet prepared to talk about.

Marina and Elarquin; what an unusual name thought Grace. They sounded lovely, Grace even thought that maybe she could meet them one day.

Grace noticed most of all when Salome spoke of her friend Alanika who now lived in Scotland, that there was a lot more she wasn't saying than what she was, she was almost dreamy when she spoke her name and Damon seemed just as affected as Salome.

They had all had a couple of red wines by now and were having a deep and meaningful conversation about life. Salome said how blessed they were to all have found their twin flames. Grace looked up as a tear rolled down her cheek and said "how lucky for you all, what do you do when your twin flame is in a higher dimension, and you can never have a physical relationship with him."

Grace couldn't believe that had just poured out of her mouth, nor the fact that she was now crying uncontrollably.

Salome went and comforted Grace.

Grace knew they would think she was an idiot.

"Is this true Grace? Grace looked at Salome and saw her sincerity, Grace nodded, it was as if she had had a truth serum and could not lie to them, no matter how much of an idiot she felt.

"You both must think I am crazy."

"Not at all, on the contrary I think you are very brave." "Brave, brave for what?"

"For having the guts to face your truth, we don't find these things out until we are ready."

"Well I don't know about that, I am still coming to terms with it, hoping it's not real, that some - how it is all a bad dream and I will wake up and find out it is not true.

I cannot believe that you could believe me so easily, that's not normal."

"Define normal for me Grace." Grace laughed, "of course it does not exist as with anything, it is in the mind of the beholder of the belief itself."

"Exactly, does this twin flame have blonde curly hair and a smile to die for?"

Grace went pale, "how do you know that?"

"He's been standing behind you all night." Damon nodded. Grace looked at them both inquisitively. "Who are you two? This is all so strange."

"Well you see, when we met Alanika, she opened up doorways of knowingness into an expanded state of consciousness for us. We both take this as a great blessing and treat it as such, although it has made our physical reality somewhat unusual. We swore to teach all we could to those who were open, that didn't mean that we couldn't still be taught, as I am learning more right now.

Grace was so relieved, she thought she would have to keep it all to herself, she excused herself and said she needed to take it all in and could they finish the conversation another time. "Of course Grace, whenever and if ever you want?" was the reply she got from Salome.

Grace had so much running through her mind that night, a part of her was so delighted to have the support of Salome and Damon, not only without judgement but also with compassionate understanding. What more could someone ask for?

Grace felt such a level of anxiety, now that she was starting to accept what was happening in her life. There was a part of her that had been yearning for this connection her whole life, and now she had it she was not sure what to do with it, where to put it in her life, the too hard box was tempting, but she knew she had gone too far now.

Aurelias had healed her heart of the hurt from her parents premature departure and she could feel that it was somewhat lighter than it had been.

It use to feel as if she was carrying around a lead weight in her chest, now it was so much lighter.

It was her mind now that was carrying the greatest burden because she just wasn't sure how to put it all together. She guessed she would just have to give it time to sort itself out.

CHAPTER 4

Grace got up early the next morning to the smell of beautiful brewing coffee. Mmm, she thought, I love that smell.

When she went to the kitchen, she saw Salome standing by the window gazing out at the ocean. Grace just stared, she looked like an angel.

"Good morning Salome." Salome nearly dropped her cup. "Oh shit, sorry, I wasn't here, I was in Scotland talking to Alanika, the fright of your voice brought me back in a hurry." "Sorry Salome, I didn't realise."

"Of course not, how could you, my body was still very much here."

"Actually I told Alanika about you and surprise, surprise she already knew," Grace looked at Salome in shock.

"What did she know?"

"She knew about you and Sorin, actually she knows you and Sorin, and you her of course.

She said her Master Zione, is your father Aurelias" Grace was speechless, is this all for real, is this really happening.

Salome smiled and went over to Grace and hugged her.

"I know how you feel Grace, I really do, I will tell you how it all came to be for me, when the time is right, but right now let's just put it all in the background and get this place ready for people, lots of people."

"What a great idea!" replied Grace with enthusiasm.

Salome held the coffee to Grace, "Here have this coffee and tell me what you think?

I thought we should try out a few for the café."

"I couldn't think of anything I would rather do right now," said Grace half to herself, she longed for earthly distraction.

"And I have the recipe here for muffins, I thought we could do savoury and sweet, first we will try the white chocolate and berry muffins."

Grace's mouth was watering at the thought of them.

Grace woke feeling very excited, the day she had dreamed of had arrived. She was finally having her opening day of the 'Lighthouse Café & Retreat' for all who wanted to expand their awareness one way or another even if it was just learning about other people in the world, other cultures and how they lived.

The Cafe had turned out beautifully, it had that Old Worldly appeal, with a touch of modern here and there.

Grace had the WiFi ready with a spare computer that anyone could use.

These were services that Grace had easy access to as a traveller and wanted to supply the same convenience for her guests, she wanted them not to have to go anywhere if they didn't want to, time to rest and integrate their journey and life if that was their desire.

Grace and Salome had done a massage course together, they thought it would be a nice service to provide if they had the time.

Grace was more interested in doing healing, she had learnt many techniques from Aurelias that she would like to use, Salome and Damon were happy to be practised on.

Grace felt a bit lonely for she had had no luck in contacting Sorin in the last couple of weeks, not even when she held her crystal, she actually felt devastated but didn't want to admit to anyone least of all herself, how cruel to love someone so much and not be able to have a physical relationship with him.

She had resigned herself to the fact of this being the way, and she knew she would rather have him in her life the way it is than not at all, so where is he? Why hasn't he come to her lately?

The opening day had turned out to be very successful. They had acquired many bookings by locals for seminars and a few

Retreats booked for different groups, Salome and Damon were as excited about it all as Grace was.

They were also glad they would have some people working for their keep because they could see that the workload would be beyond the three of them when the place was booked out, which would be quite often the way things were going.

Grace was most excited that the people wanting to stay were all happy to be vegetarian for their stay and she had the best vegetarian cook in Salome.

Grace marvelled at the wonders of the Universe, how perfect life could be when you allowed it to flow, Grace would never have been able to plan it as good as it is turning out, she had help from other dimensions and this she was very grateful for.

That night Salome cooked a beautiful Thai vegetable curry, they took it to the lighthouse and set up on the platform.

Damon carried the tables and chairs.

They thought they could do this as a special treat if it was a wedding or a birthday any special occasion that included not more than six people, it would depend on the price of the insurance!

They discussed their plans and how they would run the Guest House and Café.

Salome said she would need full time help straight away as Grace's time would be tied doing all administration duties and making sure all was running smoothly.

She was so happy she had decided to call it The Lighthouse Café & Retreat.

She had been sitting on the platform of the lighthouse one evening looking at the stars through the huge telescope that Damon and Salome had given her for an opening present, the most wonderful gift she had ever received.

She felt closer to Sorin when she stargazed. Knowing that he and Aurelias were out there somewhere on that most magical planet that was her true home, gave her peace.

Looking out to space and listening to the waves crash against the shore was a past-time she could gladly indulge herself in daily, but now that the people would be coming.

Things would change and the time she had for herself would become something of a luxury knowing she would squeeze it in every chance she got.

Salome and Damon met Grace in the community kitchen Damon had finished off.

Grace was so grateful for all Damon had been able to help her with. It took them six more weeks than Grace had anticipated, but she never expected to have the lighthouse and the community kitchen ready all at the same time.

The kitchen was really basic, an old stove, one big stainless steel bench, a big fridge and freezer and shelves for the bits and pieces, and right outside was a barbecue for the warmer months with tables and chairs made out of recycled timber from old barns and houses; they had come up beautifully.

Grace wanted her low income travellers to have some where to cook and she didn't want to have the cafe open at night, she would allow orders that they could prepare earlier and would only have to be heated up or salads that they would always have going in the cafe.

They decided to advertise the next day for a couple; a woman that could cook and help Salome in the café, and a man to help with all maintenance work and the garden.

Grace was so excited they had a group of people in from Germany. They were some sort of environmental group and were studying the Australian Flora and Fauna. This is what Grace had wanted so much, she could help them with her general knowledge of the area and she would learn so much from them in return.

She could hardly contain her excitement at the prospect of all she would be learning from her guests, she felt learning was what kept her blood flowing.

She had always been so inquisitive about any subject relating to Mother Earth and the way of humans.

It made her remember what Sorin had said about he and his kind checking the chemical levels of our oceans and forests.

It made perfect sense of course; they were part of each other, both were interested in the wellbeing of the planet and the level of awareness of its inhabitants.

Grace went and sat on the seat overlooking the sea, and stared and stared at it until she became one with it, all separation melted away as she felt one with the water and all of the creatures in it.

She felt she was the microcosm every molecule and in every drop of water, shifting to the sensation of feeling she was the macrocosm, she was the Universe and all within it, to her mind it was a contradiction, to her heart it was so wonderful so real so very very natural.

When she returned to her body she felt so clearly the limiting beliefs that we are all taught about—who and what we are. We have no chance of finding the truth until all we think we know is shattered into dust.

She knew that what was going wrong with the world was that, as a race, we had lost our connection with nature and therefore sacrificed our own authentic relationship to self.

Grace was so impressed at what had opened up in her since connecting with Sorin.

If she never saw him again she knew he had given her a gift that could last a life time.

Grace was in Istara that night in her sleep. Aurelias was teaching her about the power of crystals and how she could program them to do what she needed them to do.

Whether it be to cleanse and protect an area or to help heal blocked energy on someone.

She could hardly believe how much knowledge she could process in what seemed a short time, even though time did not exist there. This meant it may have been months in their time and five minutes in hers.

What she enjoyed the most was meeting the different beings of light that were all travelling through to other planets or dimensions. Aurelias was very well known and respected throughout many Universes. He was on a council of Masters; they made decisions that affected many races.

Grace loved him deeply and felt honoured being in his presence, and she knew her love was reciprocated.

Aurelias taught Grace how to transform peoples blocked energy in their bodies into crystalline flowing light.

The thought of being able to help people release their pain filled her with a great joy, she would help whoever she could. She had always been interested in the mystical side of life and now she was getting true understanding of it.

Although it indeed is magical there is an explanation for all things. One just needs to be able to understand one basic principal which the Scientists know, that all is energy and matter is energy vibrating at a denser slower pace, and once that vibrating goes to higher frequencies beyond the speed of light and sound all is possible.

The possibilities go beyond most humans' comprehension, and understandably so considering the limited knowledge we accumulate in our education, religious, political and social systems.

At least now there were many people choosing to look beyond the physical into the metaphysical and search for their own truths. Grace's greatest desire was to help these people have access to the information they wanted. She had never tried to push her beliefs on to anyone else though. She didn't believe anyone had the right to do this, as everyone has the right to their own beliefs.

She knew how blessed we were in Australia to be able to pursue these beliefs freely.

Grace had managed to pick up a lot of secondhand books from markets and garage sales, she had quite a collection.

She had one shelf full of travel books, she had vegetarian cook books, and of course many self help and spiritual books.

She wanted to have something for everyone, she liked the idea of people being able to take some books and read while they were staying there if that is their desire.

As Grace walked into the cafe the aroma of freshly ground coffee and muffins wafted around her, she noticed they had a few day visitors and a couple of inhouse guests eating lunch. She was so proud of Salome, her presentation was divine.

If word got around of their culinary delights, they could become quite busy as they were just on the edge of town, it was no trouble for the locals to get there.

Grace knew many would come out of inquisitiveness and then hopefully return once they learned how good the food and coffee is.

She had had a wonderful time with Salome picking out the recipes for the cafes menu. They were both more than happy with the final result.

There was a picture of the old lighthouse on the front page. Damon had done the graphic artwork and it had turned out amazing.

Grace still couldn't believe how lucky she was to have Salome and Damon helping her, they were both so very gifted in so many areas.

After the first month of being open Grace was so pleased with the takings, it was more than she could have hoped for.

She had employed a local lady to do the books twice a week and it gave Grace more time for the Café, because she loved being in there with Salome, they already had locals who were fast becoming regulars, visiting at least twice a week.

Grace had been getting up each morning and sitting on her bench overlooking the cliffs and the ocean, she never tired of the view, for every day in nature was different always. Spectacular but different in the spectrum of colours in the sky, reflecting on the ocean's surface, and the different hues of the flora depending on the shades of light and the angle of the sun, there were so many aspects that made the scenery sublime. Whether it be a calm or wild day, the wind on a bad day could cut through your skin like sharp icicles, chilling you to the bone, but still Grace found that perfect in its own way.

It turned out that Grace had no guest in for two days and she felt relieved. After six weeks of constancy, a break would be well received by Damon and Salome as well.

Salome had made the small room adjacent to the cafe into a small salon and had been doing really well with her waxing and haircuts.

Grace couldn't believe how motivated the both of them were, even though they had always managed to keep a balance. Every night they meditated and often Grace would join them.

She felt the best she had all of her life, although at night she often felt a vague restlessness, she thought it was probably due to the responsibility she now held.

She knew very well if it hadn't been for Salome and Damon she would not have coped so far, but she didn't expect them to stay for her, they had their own lives and were travelling, they would only stay for so long.

It was time Grace asked them, she had been putting it off, afraid of the answer but she would have to know so she could train someone else.

Grace was also aware of the sadness in her heart she had lost track of how long it had been since she had talked to Sorin and she had to admit to herself she missed him, she missed having the truth of what we humans have suppressed for so long, the very fact that we are so much more than we think we are, Grace had always believed it but now she had proof and as humans we need proof.

Without any consideration, Grace grabbed her crystal and focused on Sorin. As she did this she found herself looking into the wise old face of Aurelias, she smiled at the old man as her heart swelled with love.

"Where is he Aurelias, why is it so long?"

Aurelias didn't say a word, he just reached out and held Grace's hand, next thing she knew she was standing by a waterfall with Aurelias, watching in wonder as the water constantly changed colours revealing all the colours of the Rainbow and colours Grace had never seen before. She was in total awe of the ethereal majesty of the grand display, she didn't want to move in case it changed.

Her senses were having a mystical feast, she felt a tear role down her face although she was not in her physical body, it still responded to what she was feeling, she realised those sensations must have travelled through the silver chord that kept her connected to her body.

Aurelias motioned for Grace to follow him and she did. She noticed how easy they could communicate without words, she liked it, words always left out so much and paradoxically were totally superfluous.

Grace followed Aurelias as he disappeared behind the wall of water and she saw the huge entrance into the interior. She asked Aurelias where they were, and he said they were on Earth but in the fifth dimension.

Grace was humbled by the beauty and power that surrounded her, there were crystals of all colours shining brightly, hanging from the roof and woven intricately into symbols, Grace recognised from somewhere.

Aurelias told her many of the symbols were in the crop circles in England and other places in the world where they had not yet been discovered.

Grace could feel the power of the healing energies of not only the crystals but of the Sacred Geometry, she sat and felt herself sending the vibration into the cells of her body, her bones her blood. She wanted every atom of her being to be full of this beautiful healing energy.

Aurelias had to stop her, "enough Grace your body can only handle a small bit of this healing vibration at a time, other wise you can cause serious damage."

"Of course Aurelias how foolish of me to get so carried away, I so wanted my body to experience these transcendent energies, everything feels so whole and so perfect, I want everyone to experience it."

"Of course this is what we all want for humanity but free will is well and truly in place and we cannot interfere with that." "Of course not Aurelias, it would be so nice to see an end to the suffering of humanity, the darkness seems to be magnified there is so much negativity on the planet right now."

"Yes this is true, but it remains true that the greatest teacher is by example, and you have the ability and the means to do this Grace.

We have been watching your Lighthouse Retreat and wonderful things have been taking place. You might not realise it but many people there have already had major transformations taking place in their hearts and minds. This is a gift you have been able to share, with the loving support of Salome and Damon. They are the gift to you so that you may share with others."

As you know they both also are very evolved and will share more with you when the time is right, don't be afraid to share anything with either of them for they are both completely trustworthy."

"Thankyou Aurelias, I think I know this but sometimes I feel so alone in the world, even though I know I am not ever really alone, sometimes the illusion of loneliness does get the better of me."

"Yes I understand this, I have something to tell you that may change this, I know when you came to me this night you were reaching out for Sorin, am I correct?

"Yes, yes of course I was, I wanted to talk to him, to feel his energy, I miss the wholeness I feel in his presence the true unconditional love, that feeling is beyond any other I have experienced, to be known by another so completely is refreshing, it's wonderful and now I have been exposed to it I want more of it, I can't help it."

"This is a natural way for you to feel Grace, and it helps me tell you why you haven't seen Sorin for sometime.

There was a meeting with the council that overlooks Earth from a higher perspective, and it was decided that Sorin would be sent to Earth to help you because Earth is at a very serious crossroads and you need all the help and support you can get." Grace was busy ingesting what she had been told. So much was running through her mind all crashing together and making no sense.

"How, how will he do this without being too conspicuous?" "Well this is how it works Grace, he is now on the Mother Ship that sits above the Earth, he is waiting for the right time. You have probably never heard of this Grace but he is being prepared to take over another's body. This soul has fulfilled their mission on earth and was going to die, but now there has been a deal made and as his soul exits Sorin's shall enter.

During this transition he will lose a lot of his memories but not all.

He will still carry the memories and feelings of the body he will inhabit. So you see it will not be an easy process as he might not remember you at all.

But first he will have to find you. We think we can manage that part, the body is in a town not far from the lighthouse."

Grace was overwhelmed by all of this, she didn't know whether to laugh, cry, scream, she looked at the sincere face of Aurelias and knew this had to be, there was no other way, everything her and Sorin had achieved together in their many incarnations would need to be put to use if they had any chance of helping the planet and her people through this major transition.

A part of Grace felt totally elated, she would no longer be alone, she would have her love by her side, to help educate the people about how wonderful and amazing they truly are and that it is time to wake up from the deep slumber and remember who they are and what they are capable of, the thought of sharing this information made Grace want to cry, it was her whole reason for being, it was what made her feel alive, to teach and learn and experience all that she could.

"How will I know him Aurelias?"

"Well Grace, this I cannot say, for once Sorin is in the body he will be living under the rules of free will and he will have to find you naturally.

Of course there can be a small amount of divine intervention from your friends in high places." At this Aurelias laughed. Grace laughed also, what a strange predicament she had found herself in.

She spent what felt like days talking to Aurelias but when she became aware of her room it was only 3am. How could that be, she wondered until she remembered there being no time in the higher dimensions that she travelled with Aurelias.

She loved him so deeply she could have remained with him for eternity, but now she had something tangible to look forward to.

She felt a little strange about it all though. The thought of Sorin in another man's body. She was not even allowed to know what he looked like, or what he would be doing, or where they would meet.

Grace found it impossible to go to sleep that night she had so many thoughts and feelings coursing through her. She got up at the first sign of light and went and sat on her seat. It was quite chilly even though she was appropriately rugged up, she had her favourite thermals and Ugg™ boots on.

CHAPTER 5

Grace had the coffee on when Salome came in sniffing the air, "Mmm, smells good!"

Grace looked at Salome and felt herself fill with love for her, never had she had a friend as special as Salome, or as unique. Grace went to Salome and hugged her, she held so tight Salome could hardly breathe,

"Grace what's the matter, are you ok?"

"Oh Salome, I have so much to tell you, I don't know where to begin."

"Ok," said Salome, I'm all ears, fire away."

Grace proceeded to tell Salome of all that had transpired the night before. Salome sat and listened silently and at the end just said, "Wow, that's fantastic! Damon could do with another male around to help with the men's work and for a companion."

Salome for the first time told Grace how lonely Damon had been for a true friend, for he had found that in Owen and Elarquin on Magnetic Island, but they all had to go their separate ways.

Not that Damon had any trouble finding friends it was just now that he was more enlightened he found trouble finding friends on his level.

"This is wonderful news Grace, when will he be here?"

"Oh this I don't know either Salome, we have to find each other first."

Salome realised how complicated this could all be if Sorin didn't remember who Grace was. Well they would all be slightly anxious now waiting and watching all the men around to see if they could pick up any subtle similarities.

Salome was pleased that her and Damon had seen Sorin, they both felt as if they knew him and would possibly recognise his energy. Salome was glad she wasn't Grace now, she could see that she was quite distracted.

Salome could see Grace carefully studying each male that turned up. It was three weeks now since she was told of Sorin coming, but they did not mention how long or any particulars for that matter.

Grace had been trying to contact Aurelias but to no avail. She felt as if she had been left alone, she missed the depth of love that Aurelias gave her.

She was enjoying the Lighthouse Retreat enormously, there was so much sharing going on, and because of the cosy atmosphere there were many friendships being formed, this made Grace feel so content.

The cafe was doing wonderfully, there were more and more locals from the area coming along and loving the view of the ocean through the glass doors that lead out to the balcony, which would be used in spring and summer.

There was always the open fires going, people would sit in there all day, saying how much they loved the ambience.

It had worked out well having guests work for their keep, they never had to ask anyone; someone would always turn up exactly as they were required.

Grace, Damon and Salome were always so impressed by the synchronicity, all they would do is talk about what they needed and the next day there it would be. They had times where they would all get together just to give thanks for their many blessings.

Grace could hardly believe her good fortune when Salome and Damon told her that they would be more than happy to stay for at least a year.

The three of them had got together and decided it was time to start doing meditation classes. Many guests had been asking how to do it, and the three of them all had wonderful tools they could pass on.

Grace was sitting on her seat watching the ocean, she felt that beautiful feeling inside when all felt wonderful in her world. She had even managed to stop looking at every man as if they were Sorin.

She was starting to lose her focus and she could not leave all the work to Salome and Damon. So she regained her equilibrium and felt wonderful again.

She realised how important it was, no matter what was happening, to be grounded in each moment to really experience it. By wondering who and when and how all of the time she was missing the magic of being aware in each beautiful moment.

They had people from town turning up wanting to do volunteer work just to be a part of it, they could feel there was something special there but did not know what it was, except the really in tune ones, who were blown away by the spiritual openness of the three of them, Damon, Grace and Salome.

They all related their many mystical happenings as just a natural part of their daily lives and Grace was absolutely thrilled to see how many people responded to this openness by sharing their own spiritual adventures. Others just loved to listen.

Grace loved that everyone had their own special story and most of all she loved that at the Lighthouse Retreat all were treated equally.

Grace wasn't sure why but she had brought her paper and pen with her, she had no idea what to write so she just sat and meditated. The sound of the ocean's waves crashing against the shore once again lulled her into a deep peace, and then she felt the words flowing into her mind. She didn't think she just let her hand write,

My reality slips away
all I have left is the memory of you
the moon and your body glowing as one
emanating a light as bright as the sun
the ocean the wind they are all fading away my
body and all matter has gone,
nothing to hold on to, nothing to embrace
I reach out but all I find is an endless deep space
I search the Cosmos looking for you
where are you my love, I know you are there,
somewhere
My mind reaches out beyond the stars,
I search and search for you for nowhere seems too
far and then I remember to think of home
for the thought itself is my map
it shows me a pattern of a planet where I belong
and this is where I shall find you my love
for this is our song, a song shared for aeons of time
a song that will always be yours and mine
I shall wait now for you in the rocks and the sand
I shall wait for you in the trees and the wind
I shall wait for you in the place of our first birth
I shall wait for you now on planet Earth.

When Grace finished she had no idea what she had written, but she felt as if she had been on a long journey, the words somehow transported her beyond time and space. It had left her feeling somewhat peculiar, and then she read the words....

The tears were streaming down her face as she felt her heart expand, there was so much truth in her words they rocked her world.

It gave her a deep knowing of something she had not understood before.

Those words obviously came from her superconscious self, or higher self, whatever people liked to call it, it didn't really matter, it is that part of us all that knows all, that is all, that part that most humans have forgotten about.

Grace felt the tears streaming down her face, her heart felt big enough to encompass every being in existence, she was completely overwhelmed by her heart's capacity to love in such an expanded state, and her awareness, knowingness matched the love she felt. 'My cup runneth over.' Now she knew exactly how that felt.

There was no beginning and no end just one Grand constantly expanding infinite now.

CHAPTER 6

Grace was sitting in the cafe with Salome, she was looking at one of the bare walls, wondering what she could do with it. Salome said, "why don't you get a mural painted on it, something really special?"

Grace pondered over the suggestion for a while imagining what it would look like and most of all what could be painted there. She decided she liked the idea and they could all get together and work out what would look really amazing there. She wanted something that made people feel good.

Grace showed what she had written to Salome, when Salome read it, Grace saw the tear slide down her cheek. "It reminds me of another poem I read once, by someone I love very dearly.

Grace that is beautiful, I know it has been some time now since you have had contact but this must restore your faith that all is as it should be."

"Yes Salome, you are right about that, my anxiety has fallen away and been replaced with a huge resounding trust in the greater plan.

Although I have no idea when I will see Sorin again, it is comforting to know that we have a deep connection with Mother Earth and her evolution.

Now I just have this overpowering feeling to experience and share as much as I can with all of those out there who are awake."

"Yes, I agree it is such an exciting time to be on this planet, so many are realising our cosmic connection to other star systems and Universes. The reality of who we are and what we are is infinite; what a great joy this is to embrace.

Well Grace it is opening time, let's share the joy of this great awareness we are constantly discovering!"

"Yes let's!" responded Grace feeling totally inspired.

The girls got extra creative with their food and started making biscuits in shapes of angels and stars. People responded to it, it gave them a distraction from the heaviness that many were experiencing in their daily lives.

Metaphysically speaking it was an amazing time, but physically it was very challenging because our bodies are so dense due to the many generations of suffering mentally, emotionally, spiritually and physically. Grace believed these old patterns were transforming, but at this stage the process was rather painful and many were suffering without understanding why—hence the overwhelming amount of people turning to anti-depressants and anything else that could take them away from what they were feeling.

Just to numb a pain that they didn't understand and because they were living in a society that so easily says, block it out! Don't work your way through it, that's impossible.

This is why Grace loved meditating so much, it gave her a deep knowing that all she was experiencing had a higher purpose and all could be worked through if one was prepared to trust the process.

Grace woke up with a strange feeling like butterflies in her solar plexus. It gave her that sense of anticipation, for what she had no idea, she could not recall any of her dreams but maybe that was where the feeling had come from.

She went into the cafe and turned on the coffee machine, she wanted a real coffee, it was only 6.30am and all the guests were still in their rooms, not surprising considering it felt about 1 degree outside.

Grace sat staring at the empty wall still trying to decide what to have painted there, while she was waiting for the coffee machine to warm up.

And then suddenly she could see it, flowers, trees, the rainbow waterfall she had been to with Aurelias, she could see it as if it were alive, real.

The crystal cave she could see it all alive on her wall. It was so real it made her heart beat fast and tears roll down her cheeks. How could she get someone to capture that beauty, that absolute magnificent display of divinity in form? She could hear Aurelias's words in her mind. "What you are seeing is quite real, there is a reason why this wall has been chosen it sits on a portal through to the dimension that you experienced with me and when people see this mural they will be transported there and all of their senses will pick up on the vibrational level and start remembering who they are, for this beauty is a part of them all on other levels."

Grace woke Salome and Damon up and told them about her revelations regarding the painting. They both felt excited about it, now all they needed to do was to find an artist that had the ability to tap into the other dimensions and bring it through.

Salome had an idea and rang Sarah for she had many arty friends in the city, surely one would be inspired by a free stay in a guesthouse overlooking the ocean, with beautiful vegetarian food in constant supply.

Sarah said she knew of someone who had the talent but he had been through a really tough time and she did not know if he was up to it, still she passed on his number to Salome to give him a go.

His name was Matthew Mason and he was 39 years old. Salome had a good feeling about Matthew and rang him immediately.

He was hesitant for some time but then finally decided to give it a go, if Damon would pick him up.

Salome wasn't sure why but he sounded paranoid about going on his own, and then she remembered what Sarah said about him going through a really tough time.

Salome rang Sarah back just to check that he was suitable, they could do without some wierdo hanging around, it wouldn't be good with the guests.

Sarah told Salome that he had never really fitted in with society and people in general. He was an eccentric loner.

Salome was a little worried, she didn't want to bring anyone in that would upset any of the guests, or most of all Grace.

She knew she could rely on Damon, he would know if it was worth giving him a go as soon as he met him.

Now they just had to tell Grace that Damon would be going to get him the next day.

Grace was surprised that they had found someone so soon, but they wouldn't know if he was up to the task until he was there, at the worst he would get a free holiday.

Grace gave Salome the day off as well, she didn't want Damon going on his own, they were so good to Grace.

They had a couple of women from the town they could call on at short notice, and Grace was looking into giving unemployed young people a go, she wanted to give them free training and hopefully help improve their self-esteem.

She knew how easy it was to get down on yourself when you had no money or job prospects, she had experienced it first hand, now she had the means she would help as many as she could gain confidence and she had the full support of Salome and Damon.

Salome didn't have the qualifications for cooking to teach someone professionally although she had a lot of knowledge and skills to share and the same went for Damon, he could teach the young boys many skills that would be very handy in their work or personal life.

CHAPTER 7

alome was looking at Matthew wondering how Grace would respond to him, he had long blonde dreadlocks, his eyebrow pierced and many tattoos, he was quite handsome thought Salome in a broody sort of way, he hardly spoke unless he was spoken to, he was definitely in his own world.

Salome almost felt sorry for him, he had a sensation of being lost emanating around him, Salome found herself wanting to protect him from the world, he seemed somewhat overwhelmed by everything.

It was a long trip back, Damon had even given up trying to have a conversation, Matthew's answers were short and severe; he didn't want to talk that was obvious.

When they arrived at the Lighthouse Salome saw a spark in Matthew's eyes, they were a beautiful deep green.

So he likes it here she thought, at least that was one thing. He was getting his paints out, when Grace arrived, she was talking to Salome and Damon about the ten guests that were to show up at any minute.

Matthew turned around and stood up, he was about six foot three, he towered over Grace.

Grace caught his eye and they were fixed on each other, as if some magnet were holding them together.

Grace held her hand out and felt a slight tingle when they touched.

Matthew quickly excused himself and returned to fetching the rest of his belongings.

Damon took Matthew and showed him to his room and left him there, he would be staying in the main homestead, where Grace, Salome and he slept. It was really quite large and they could keep out of each others way.

At sunset Grace looked out the window to see Matthew approaching the Lighthouse, he was most certainly an enigma, Salome and Damon could not even work him out and they were both very intuitive.

Damon so hoped that Matthew was up to the job, if not it was a lot of time and money wasted, instinctively deep down he felt a connection to Matthew although he had no idea what that connection was.

Matthew was extremely reticent, it would take a long time to get anything personal out of him; if ever.

Well Damon was not one to give in that easily, he always had people open up to him about their lives. Things they could not tell other people, for some reason they felt safe with him, so hopefully he would have the same effect on Matthew.

He would take him to the surf beach tomorrow and watch the Pro surfers, Damon loved to watch them, they were so skilled and fearless, and it was a good excuse for him to sit and stare at the ocean which he loved to do, it was a bit cold for him to go in at the moment.

He looked forward to swimming with Salome, he loved her so much, he decided when the time was right he would ask her to marry him, he had never loved anyone the way he loved Salome, they had been together for eighteen months now, and she was still a delightful mystery to him and he was more than happy for it to stay that way.

She had remained fiercely independent and unique. Most girls he met changed once they were together for a while, all they wanted to do was settle down, but not Salome, she hadn't changed at all and she asked almost nothing of him, she totally allowed him to be himself, it was lovely.

He really did not know whether she wanted a legal binding but there was only one way he could find out and he was happy to put his ego on the line and take the risk.

Grace walked over to the window and looked at the ocean in the moonlight. She marvelled at the fact that never once did it appear the same. She could hear the waves as she opened the window, oh, how she loved that sound.

She stood listening, and then she noticed there was a candle burning in the Lighthouse. That's strange who would be there this time of night she wondered, it was out of bounds for the guests unless Grace, Salome or Damon were there, the stairs were quite dangerous and Grace's insurance would hit the roof if there were any accidents.

Grace had to wipe her eyes, she saw the ship hovering over the Lighthouse, so you are still there, although he is not she thought.

She hadn't met them yet, but in her heart she knew she loved them and they would show themselves when the time was right, and Sorin had said they were family, which means they were somehow connected to Aurelias also.

She saw bright deep pink and blue lights shooting out in all directions, she laughed thinking what if the guests were watching, they were getting one hell of a show.

But somehow she knew they were there for her to reassure her that she wasn't alone, she had come to treasure their presence and would look forward to meeting them.

She noticed the candle went out and then she saw a torch light headed toward her house, she was straining trying desperately to see who was there, her breath caught when she saw the long dreadlocks swaying in the wind, she hadn't noticed before but he walked as if his feet barely touched the ground, almost gliding. Who was this Matthew? Well she intended on making it her mission to find out, all she had to do was to get him to open up. She would find his passion that always worked.

Well maybe she already knew, painting possibly was his passion, she would show him tomorrow what she wanted and see if he could do it. It was a big job and just maybe he had what was necessary to tap into the higher dimensions and bring through the absolute beauty that exists there.

Grace went back to bed and sent her love to the ship and whomever was on it, she felt the love immediately returned ten fold, it made her heart skip a beat, she was anxious to make their acquaintance as no other.

Just as she was almost asleep she saw the most beautiful face appear before her, well not exactly a face more like light; beautiful pastel coloured light in the shape of a face that appeared male/female in one.

The most intense golden eyes looked at her and filled her with a knowing, a knowing that all was indeed changing in her world and the world around her.

Next thing she knew she was looking into a huge crystal that was in the middle of a room in a massive ship. She knew it was the one she had been seeing. At last she thought. Although part of her felt strange, mostly she felt right at home.

She was watching different scenes that must have been taking place right now, it was like the crystal was shooting out light toward the different screens and there were a multitude of situations taking place simultaneously.

Grace was baffled she had no idea what was going on, trying to integrate all that was occurring, which was overwhelming her. "What you are witnessing Grace is the plight of humans. They are so far off track again. Their egos, which are based on illusion, are ruling their lives and creating their realities, they live in so much fear due to their media, social belief systems and of course consensus reality.

They live as if life is a constant competition, always competing and trying to be the best. The only true measurement of their lives is their personal growth, which all takes place within and is unique to all, and the ability to open their hearts to an authentic way of life and live without limitations, constantly expanding their awareness of reality and existence of all life. This is where they can experience the true meaning of joy!" The beautiful face disappeared, but somehow Grace knew she stayed with the light being who she learnt was Stariam and he continued to share his wisdom with her, which was an infinite source of knowledge and wisdom of this Universe and many others.

When Grace got up the next morning she felt disdain and elation wrestling inside of her. The extreme disdain she felt was for the mess we humans had gotten ourselves into.

We have managed to treat our beloved Earth as if she were something to be raped and pillaged daily, we take her gems, her minerals, everything we can to help with our technical 'so called' evolution when indeed the only thing it is sure to bring is destruction. You see we don't learn from our mistakes; we just alter them slightly to make ourselves believe we have learnt and changed but we are repeating history no matter how we look at it.

Other civilisations had found themselves in the greedy destructive seat we are sitting in now and it was the end for them…it was their demise.

The elation came from the knowledge that Grace had finally met Stariam and had been shown by Stariam that we can still turn this around by creating our own beautiful reality, the pain and suffering is an illusion that humans had become addicted to, coming back time and time again to make the same mistakes.

It is time we jump off the wheel of karma and create our own amazing blessed reality. All one has to do is be prepared to release the dramas in one's head and one's life, the deeply seated addiction to suffering.

So many people say I don't want dramas, and maybe that's true, but everyone must take full responsibility for their realities; know they are the creator of their own reality and turn it around into something that makes them proud, a conscious manifested reality of beauty and love something that will roll into eternity with Divine Grace.

Grace knew now with every fibre of her being that she had created all of her life; together with the others that played their parts, they all had chosen what they needed to learn.

It felt so empowering not to feel one bit of a victim and to know she had chosen on some level everything she had experienced so far.

It made so much sense and yet was so far removed from what we are brought up to believe.

Grace took a deep breath and thanked Stariam for reminding her of the Grand infinite truth of life, the miracle that indeed we are our own creators. When we accept that responsibility consciously we are free. Grace felt as if a huge light had been switched on inside her and she didn't ever want it to turn off, now she knew her family was whole.

CHAPTER 8

Grace sat and ate breakfast on her own. She was feeling deeply introspective, so much had been revealed to her in such a short time, she needed to find a place for it all, and somehow remain grounded.

She could still feel Stariam's love surrounding her, it was so beautiful, there was a part of her that wanted to stay with him but she knew it was not time, she had a purpose to fulfil on Earth as everyone does and she would be with her true family soon enough.

Until then it was back to business. She decided it was time to get Matthew and see if he was up to the task of painting the mural as it existed in the fifth dimension.

Grace was sitting looking out to sea when she heard the door open, she turned to see Matthew enter, he had his paints in one hand and a canvas floor mat in the other.

Grace felt so impressed by his intuitiveness, he acknowledged her with a slight nod and started setting up.

Grace was speechless he was so intent on what he was doing he failed to see her gobsmacked face.

He turned and looked at her and said "I hope you will be closed for the next week, it would be a little difficult with distractions."

"Of course, whatever you need," Grace replied with a slight smile, she liked this stranger more than she was willing to admit.

She opened her mouth to tell Matthew what she wanted the mural to be, but no words would form in her mind she had hit a total blank.

She watched Matthew totally absorbed in getting prepared, she knew now that whatever he painted was what was meant to be, she had to trust his own creativity, although she had not witnessed any of his former work.

Grace asked Matthew if he would like a cup of coffee, but he declined, he was on a mission thought Grace and it was time to leave him to it. Although she felt a little anxious, she had to trust him.

Grace managed to delay all bookings for a week, they all needed a rest.

Grace would watch Matthew go to the cafe every morning at 6am and he would be there until well after dark.

After the fourth day she was starting to become way to curious to wait any longer, she found an excuse to have to go to the cafe, it was a legitimate excuse, she did need to start cooking. Salome was just as eager to see what Matthew had created, she was also excited that they had some Scottish people coming to stay who had just spent a month with Alanika and Owen. Just thinking of them brought tears to her eyes. Although she could speak to Alanika it was mostly telepathically and on occasion Alanika had appeared before her for a very brief moment, but it was not the same as being in the flesh with her.

Damon had told her that he wanted to go and stay with them in Scotland after they had done a year with Grace at the Guesthouse. She was so excited she could barely contain herself, she felt as if she were bursting out of her skin.

Three whole months in the Scottish Highlands with her beloved soul family, what a treat, she was so proud of Owen for taking his new found destiny in his stride and he was excelling at sharing his knowledge and love for the Earth, and teaching the young people he had met during his many years of travelling with no particular purpose except to have a good time.

Now they were drawn to go and stay with Owen and Alanika, and Salome could only imagine what Alanika would be sharing with them, she had taught Salome and Marina so much and Salome loved the thought of others having access to the magic that was Alanika from the stars.

Salome visualised Alanika shining her beautiful light on all that walked through her doorway, helping them to remember how amazing they all are.

Salome was smiling when Grace appeared before her, "hi Salome,"

"Hi Grace, nice to see you, where are you going?"

"I am just heading into town to get some supplies for the Scottish guests, there will be six of them and we need all fresh supplies; due to us not using the cafe for four days."

"Yes, of course we will, would you like me to come along and help?"

"That would be great Salome, I would really appreciate the company, I can't explain it but I have been feeling a bit strange since Matthew started the mural, maybe it's just the curiosity.

I am not sure, you see I did not even tell him what I want, I couldn't, the words just wouldn't come out so I had to trust in his natural instinct, or intuition more likely."

Salome smiled and held out her hand to Grace, "don't worry Grace, I am sure all will be fine, we will find out soon enough anyway because we will have to go to the cafe with the new supplies."

Grace smiled and thanked Salome, they talked about Matthew and how elusive he was. They had hardly laid eyes on him since he had been painting.

Damon had kept himself busy fixing bits and pieces and sprucing up the website.

Grace and Salome walked up to the Cafe with their groceries.

Grace could feel herself shaking, don't be silly she thought it is just a painting after all.

They knocked on the door, and could hear muffled sounds, and finally the door opened, Grace could not believe the transformation in Matthew's face, he looked illumined she just stared and had no words, the silence was finally broken when Matthew said, "I'm not quite finished yet but you are both welcome to come in."

Thank goodness thought Salome these groceries are starting to become somewhat heavy.

Grace stepped in first. She looked straight over at the wall as the tears filled her eyes and her heart thudded loudly, so loud she could hear her own blood pumping through her body. Everything around her disappeared as she felt herself standing in the picture, the likeness was entrancing, the waterfall the colours emanating off in all directions in sprays of water, and behind was a cave with crystals. He had somehow managed to make it look three dimensional, but what took her breath away was the old man with the long grey beard holding a white dove on his palm, he had a long white robe on, his likeness to Aurelias was phenomenal.

There were flowers and trees and everything Grace had envisaged, she had to remind herself to breathe, she had been holding her breath without realising.

Salome was blown away by the Ethereal beauty Matthew had captured, she couldn't take her eyes off it, especially the old man, she felt as if she knew him, she felt the wisdom of his presence; an ancient wisdom reaching through time and space eradicating all illusion!

Matthew watched the girls respond to his picture, he was a bit overwhelmed by the affect it seemed to be having on them, especially Grace.

He liked what he had done, but had not expected this reaction. Grace looked at Matthew and was totally speechless, she stood patiently waiting for the words to form, eventually the words "I like your work" came out...well that was the understatement of the century!

Oh Matthew, this is perfect how can I thankyou, I didn't expect something as beautiful as this.

Matthew blushed he wasn't used to such a warm reception to his work, there were a lot of good artists around these days, one needed to be exceptional to be able to make a living out of it.

Grace could see that Matthew had no idea at the magnificence he had created on her wall, to him it was just a painting but to Grace it was so much more.

All was silent for some time, before Salome said, "well I'm going to put these groceries away, I have some serious cooking to do."

Grace couldn't pull herself away from the painting.

Finally she managed to drag herself to the coffee machine and switch it on. "You must be hungry Matthew, would you like a coffee and something to eat?"

"I would love that Grace, I have been so absorbed in the mural I have hardly been sleeping or eating, it is strange but I have not found that I needed to."

Grace smiled at him, she wanted to hug him but found herself resist, he wasn't ready for that sort of affection she could feel it.

"Well Matthew, I am overwhelmed by your talent." Matthew smiled shyly, Grace could see he wasn't use to compliments.

Grace said, "seriously Matthew I had no idea at the extent of your talent, I feel a couple of weeks free board isn't nearly sufficient for what you have accomplished, is there anything else you would like?"

"Well actually, yes there is, I have no plans and no home right now, so I was wondering if maybe you would have a job for me, I really love it here, there is something that feels right to me and I would like to explore that a little longer if I could have the opportunity."

Grace looked at Matthew and somehow felt relieved she wanted him to stay not knowing exactly why but she needed him there. "Of course you can have work here, Damon is always busy and I am sure he could do with a hand."

"Absolutely," Salome added, "he would love to have a man around to help him"

Matthew felt so relieved he liked these people and he had no idea where his life was taking him before he got that phone call from Sarah.

He had a home at least for a while anyway, long enough to get some money together and work out what to do next.

Matthew felt comfortable working while the girls were chattering away and many lovely smells started wafting out from the kitchen, he hadn't realised how hungry he was until then.

Salome walked out with a plate with steaming hot muffins, she handed it to him, "here eat this and tell me what you think." Matthew looked at the butter melting and was sure he was drooling, he sat down and then Grace handed him a mug of freshly brewed coffee, "thank you Grace."

Grace looked at him as he smiled at her and a moment of recognition passed between them. It was gone as quickly as it had come.

CHAPTER 9

Grace felt strange that night. She kept reliving that moment that Matthew smiled at her and that feeling of recognition she had experienced. Surely she would have remembered if she had met him, he had the most amazing green eyes. She wanted to stare at him. He was quite shy, he didn't have the confidence he deserved.

Still Grace found his humble manner very attractive, yes she was falling for this Matthew no mistake, she was trying to stop the feelings for she knew she had to wait for Sorin to find her, and then finally the bell went off, OMG he could be Sorin, now her thoughts were going crazy.

What if he is? How could she be certain if he doesn't remember?

There would have to be a sign, maybe the mural is a sign, his ability to capture higher dimensions, but then people did that all the time.

She dedicated her night to her thoughts, much to her disdain, and still she had no clear answer. All the questions swirling in her mind with no clarity to be found. She was tired and cranky when she finally found her way to the kitchen. She turned the coffee on and realised the Scottish would be there in four days. She had so much to do!

The Scottish came and went, they all had the most fabulous time. Laughing, eating, sharing intimate stories, there were some really solid bonds formed.

Even Matthew joined in, he didn't say much, but all enjoyed his company.

He even took them on a bush walk, he had considerable knowledge of the flora and fauna. This impressed Grace so deeply, she asked him if he would make the bush walk a permanent activity.

He smiled at Grace as if she had offered him the world which, she was beginning to realise, she would if she possibly could. Damon and Salome had made arrangements to meet the Scottish visitors in Scotland at their mutual friend's guest house in the Highlands.

Grace and Matthew were invited to go along also. Grace was tempted, she had heard so much about Alanika and Owen she felt like she knew them; which of course she did on some level of awareness, considering Aurelias had been Alanika's Master teacher.

She could not see herself leaving the lighthouse for some time, it was going so well she didn't want to change the direction it was heading in…but it was indeed tempting!

There were a couple of weeks ahead without any bookings, Grace decided to give Salome and Damon a nice break, if they wanted it, they certainly had earned it.

Grace would have no trouble running the café with some of the girls from town.

Matthew would be able to do the day-to-day chores that Damon usually handled.

Grace had been lying in bed thinking of Matthew, she could not get his face out of her mind, always those beautiful deep green eyes, which had such a light shining out of them. They made Grace catch her breath.

Salome and Damon happily took Grace up on her offer, they wanted to go for a camping trip to the mountains of North East Victoria. Salome wanted to show Damon where she had spent some time in her youth with a wonderful lady named Deidre. Deidre had taught Salome about the healing properties of herbs, before her mother so rudely dragged her off…as usual!

Salome also knew it was time Grace and Matthew had some time alone, there was some connection there that needed to be explored, and they both knew Grace was secretly hoping Matthew was Sorin…it was time she found out!

Salome and Damon had gone, and Grace decided to give the others a day off. She desperately needed time to herself, time to sit and stare at the sea and release all earthly responsibilities. Time to contemplate all that they had achieved so far.

Grace was walking toward her seat when she spotted Matthew already there. She went to turn and walk away but something stopped her and pushed her in his direction, she hoped she was imagining it, but knew she was not, there was a force pushing her toward him as if he were a magnet.

She approached apprehensively and asked if she could join him. He moved over and said, "of course Grace, I have been waiting for you."

Grace felt her whole body heat up and sweat form on her brow.

She sat and for some time they stared in companionable silence watching the waves of the ocean crashing in against the cliff's edge relentlessly. Such great power, thought Grace. She tried to put the strength inside of her, she needed it, she needed to have the strength to find out what was inside of Matthew. Did he have the same feelings as she, or was she being fanciful hoping that he was Sorin.

Matthew put his hand out searching for Grace's. As soon as she felt it she responded and held his.

"This is hard for me Grace, I have never been good at sharing my feelings, but I am aware there is something tangible between us, something I would very much like to explore further."

Grace felt so relieved that Matthew had broken the ice and taken the first step in an intimate conversation.

"Something strange has happened to me Grace, you will think I am crazy, but I feel like I am two people in one body, it is scaring me because I do not know how to control or understand it."

Grace looked at Matthew full of empathy for his situation, at the same time she felt so relieved, she was scared to believe it, but now she was quite sure he was her Sorin.

Matthew turned and looked into Grace's eyes, he could see that they were filling with tears.

"I am sorry Grace, I did not mean to alarm you." "It's not that Matthew, I owe you a story."

Grace told Matthew everything that had happened since she took over the Guest house, all of her meetings with Sorin.

Her journeys with Aurelias, she told him everything. He listened intently not saying a word.

Grace said "I am so sorry I should have said something sooner, I was worried you would have thought I was a nutcase."

"Grace this all sounds crazy, but I believe you, I have to, it is the only explanation that makes sense to the contradictions I have been experiencing, it has been so damned complicated.

I am a simple man with simple needs, all of a sudden I have this higher information coming to me and I do not know what to do with it.

Knowledge I have never contemplated before."

They sat in silence integrating all that they were acknowledging, it all felt so surreal, they were both completely entranced watching the ocean, time stood still as they became one.

They were still holding hands when Grace's awareness returned. They looked into each others eyes and searched for themselves, trying to understand the feelings that swept them up, the feeling of being one, not separate, never separate.Grace got up and said, "I need to go back to the house, I feel so strange, would you like to join me?"

Matthew felt like he should be saying more, he was so overcome with emotion, he felt he was holding back a life time of tears and loneliness.

Sorin had no idea how to deal with all the sad memories of pain and sorrow that were in the cells of the body he had walked into.

The love he was feeling for Grace was so powerful that it seemed to push out all of those years of pain and abandonment, that Matthew had experienced due to a very neglectful upbringing, devoid of love and caring.

This was going to be so much harder than either of them had anticipated. Only love could bring them through this crazy situation together, and that they had in spades.

Grace took Matthew to her bedroom, neither felt safe to face any earthly situations right now, they were both raw and vulnerable, especially Matthew.

Grace lay on top of the bed and Matthew followed, they just held each other, looking into the other's eyes, both crying softly.

Here they were together at last, it was so intense neither could speak, they went to sleep this way and didn't wake up till the morning.

CHAPTER 10

M atthew went and checked all the rooms and made some final adjustments, they had some guests arriving the next day.

Grace was keeping herself busy in the kitchen, she couldn't believe how much she enjoyed baking.

Salome had taught her in such a casual fashion, she caught on quite easily.

She made sultana muffins as well as savoury muffins, she used gluten free flour as it was in high demand these days, nearly every group that came had at least one gluten free person in it. Most of the backpackers were vegan or vegetarian, which was a good thing.

Grace was never much of a meat eater so had many recipes and ideas for food she could make.

She made herself a coffee and sat and stared at the mural Matthew painted on the wall, she was so startled at the likeness to the astral dimension she had travelled to with Aurelias.

Before she knew it she found herself by the waterfall with Aurelias, "greetings daughter," "and to you father" they placed their hands on each others hearts and put their third eyes together.

With a flash of light Grace found herself walking deep into the cave behind the waterfall. There were crystals of all colours everywhere, reds, greens, pinks, blues and many clear quartz, all emitting a gentle glow bright enough for Grace to see.

Grace felt as if she was being called deeper and deeper into the cave, she followed, somehow her heart was pulling her.

She could hear soft music and the sensation of recognition touched her senses.

Although she was not in her physical body she was aware of her heart beating loud and fast, anticipation and excitement were pulling her forward, and then suddenly she was stopped by a power that nearly knocked her over, she looked around and she was completely alone, Aurelias was gone.

She saw where the power was coming from, it was a life size crystal ball, the energy around it was pulsing outward in waves, Grace could barely contain the power it emitted.

She heard a beautiful female voice telling her to come closer. Grace was mesmerised as she looked into the massive crystal, and the voice said, I am the essence of your mother planet, I live in the body of every person on earth…just as you all have an eternal essence and a soul in your body, I too have a soul that resides in my body.

Grace could feel a powerhouse of emotion take over her being. She watched the crystal as she saw pictures form in it. They were scenes of women, old, young, mothers with their babies suckling at their breasts, the old crone fetching herbs in the bush, High Priestesses in times Grace was not familiar with, dressed in garb that she had never seen before.

She saw modern day women dressed up to please men, she saw whores selling their bodies.

And then the voice said, "this is what some of your women of today have declined to, using their bodies for attention in the hope that it will bring them love; but only misery can come from such a misguided intention.

For true love is unconditional and comes from a love that is based on soul connection and mutual respect for one another. She saw men blowing holes in the planet, putting poison and bombs inside her, with no awareness of the pain they were causing this loving being whom we call Mother Earth.

She witnessed children treating their mothers most unkindly. Men abusing their rights of matrimony.

She saw land being plundered for oil and gold and various other minerals.

Grace called out "stop" please, she fell to the ground with loud resounding sobs releasing from her soul.

Her heart felt it was bleeding.

Why, why have humans become so vile, so ignorant to your power of love and the many blessings you bestow upon us. Grace felt a nurturing love embrace her and remove all her judgement.

The lovely voice said "my dear judging is not the way to change, you must see the beauty firstly in yourselves and in your fellow human, and then you will have the ability to transform and recognize that the beauty in nature that you are constantly surrounded by, is but a reflection of your own beauty.

You are all loved beyond your own imaginations but you have lost the ability to experience this love, to allow it to permeate your being, to express it in your everyday activities, to bring you knowledge and the true history of your planet, for there have been many other civilisations on this planet that you have no recollection of.

You have become blinded as a race always in search for personal power and riches. You are losing your ability to connect to nature and in losing this connection you are losing the connection to your own authentic life path.

My body is in pain Grace and my heart breaking for my children who have lost their way."

"Hold out your hand Grace." Grace did this and she saw the most stunning female face appear in the crystal. Grace felt frozen, never had she seen anything so striking.

The face had flowers and fields, mountains, oceans, deserts, rivers, lakes, and then she saw the darkness appear working its way through and a lone tear came out of the infinite eyes of the majestic Mother Earth, they were the most lovely vibrant blue/green, Grace felt the tear on her palm.

"This is the tear of your Mother Earth. It is sacred and has been entrusted to you Grace to let it guide you on your chosen path, there is much power in this tear drop, for it is the essence of every tear that has fallen on your planet from all women suffering the same fate as I, rape and ignorance to your divine inner beauty.

You now have your true partner who shall honour you and all women, in the most sacred of ways.

Grace felt something cool on her hand and saw that a lovely crystal had formed around the tear in the shape of the tear drop.

"You have chosen the path Grace, to contribute in awakening humanity to their beauty and divinity."

Grace didn't feel like she could take anymore, the pain and the love were so great so contradictory and also tangible.

Go now Grace, and remember I am always with you, you have much to do."

Grace felt shell shocked she just stood and next thing she knew she was coming back to consciousness sitting in her café looking at her mural.

She thought she must have surely been dreaming, although her feelings were saying otherwise.

She opened her hand and there it was, the crystal with the earth mother's tear drop in it.

Grace cried until she was sobbing, how could she feel so much pain and so much love at the same time.

One thing she knew is she would honour the great mother's

wishes and do all she could to help awaken anyone who was open or at least ready to be open.

Grace slipped into a deeply quiet place within her and heard theses words:

> I am divine
> The essence of your planet
> I am cosmic and universal
> I am one with the creator of life
> I am love that floats on a summer breeze
> I am joy that sings through your trees
> I am animals wild and tame
> I am birds flying through the sky
> I am the beauty and scent within your colourful flowers
> I am the power that sits in your mountains
> I am the bubbles that flow through waterfalls
> I am the stillness that sits in your lakes
> I am the joy that sings through your heart when you awaken
> I am the blessings in your fruits
> I am the one that loves you through eternity
> We will always be linked you and me
> So spread your wings and let your soul fly free
> I am you and you are me!

CHAPTER 11

Grace and Matthew were having a lovely time getting to know each other.

Matthew was still struggling with two levels of consciousness: Sorin's higher understanding of life and the cosmos, and Matthew's human pain of the past, which was recorded in all of his cells as is with all humans.

Matthew was working very hard at finding a place within himself where these two incongruous energies could work together in harmony.

It was a work in progress, but he felt that he was definitely making progress. He only had flashes and insights of Sorin's knowledge, mostly he was experiencing the human which was appropriate considering that was the dimension he was vibrating in.

He and Grace were very excited at the prospect of humans merging with the higher consciousness. Now the crossroads were well and truly open so all of this was not only possible but a collective probability for the whole human race.

The beauty of experiencing nature as a multi-dimensional creation had been beyond Grace's wildest dreams, but this was how it was for her now that Matthew had painted the mural and added a doorway into the higher dimensions. This mural had also allowed everybody who came to the café to have a multi-dimensional experience if they wanted it, and were ready for it.

Grace and Matthew's souls would be the guardians that allowed others safe passage into the other dimensions.

Grace wanted to make sure this would not happen for people spontaneously, she would have the meditation classes in the café in the evenings, so all could be prepared for their journey.

What an amazing gift Aurelias had passed on to humanity. It was his deep love for Mother Earth and her loving creations that inspired him as an evolved being to continue to work with the evolution of human consciousness!

Grace had not shared with Matthew yet what had transpired in the cave with the Earth Mother essence.

Matthew, Grace could see, was working so hard to find a place within him where all somehow made sense, she was proud of him – he was doing an amazing job.

They had not made love yet. Aurelias told Grace it was important not to, as humans had lost the ability to bond on an energetic level first, connecting their heart centres and expanding that into their higher chakras.

This way they would have total respect for each other, and the ability to trust each other completely.

So they meditated together connecting all of their chakras, which of course are all aspects of themselves.

Following lust only leads to dis-integration, where as connecting hearts leads to total integration.

Matthew and Grace were sitting in the café having a coffee and looking out the glass doors toward the ocean. They could both feel a buzz in the air as if something was about to happen, feeling anticipation for something, but they had no idea what. They were discussing this feeling, trying to locate where it was coming from.

All was going so well at the Guest House, they had made many new friends all who were conscious of the changes they were needing to address in their lives, to feel more connected to nature and in turn to their true authentic selves.

They had been able to share much knowledge of the metaphysical aspects of awareness, and had learnt much with what had been shared with them.

They knew that all were equal in the eye of the Creator and all had a gift to share, being an aspect of the Creator. They did their best to help others find and open up to their gifts as Mathew and Grace were constantly learning more and opening more of their gifts.

They had decided to close the café on Mondays. They needed one day to catch up on the cooking in the café and other chores that had been neglected due to having people stay back to back for the past month.

They heard a car pull up and looked at each other, neither were in the mood for idol chatter, they were so enjoying their quiet time together.

The café door opened and there was Salome, she ran over to them, they got up and hugged each other, it had turned into two months, and here they were.

Damon strolled in with a huge smile on his face he walked over and embraced them both.

They were all so happy, Grace could see a change in Salome and Damon.

Salome held out her left hand and there was a beautiful sapphire and diamond ring shining on her wedding finger. Grace squealed she was so excited, "oh my what wonderful news." Salome smiled calmly and said, "we have so much to tell you, we ended up going back to Magnetic Island where we met, and Damon proposed to me on a rock overlooking the sea, it was so romantic."

Salome and Damon looked at Matthew as he put his arm around Grace and they could all feel the love between them, it was electric.

Damon said, "it looks like we all have a lot of catching up to do."

They could not believe the difference in Matthew, he felt like a completely different person.

Salome said, "the best surprise is yet to come, we have decided to get married here, if that is ok with the two of you?"

Grace was so thrilled, she put her hand out to Salome and said, "there is nothing I would rather than to have you married here, what a blessing for us all."

Salome said, "Damon go get our friends." Grace looked as Salome said, "you will never guess what? We hope you don't mind us bringing them with us, if it is ok they are going to stay for a couple of weeks.

They will help out with whatever they can."

"Of course they can," said Grace enthusiastically. Matthew and her looked at each other and knew where the buzz had been coming from.

Grace and Matthew looked toward the door as Damon walked in. Behind him was a beautiful girl with golden red wavy hair to her thighs.

Damon said, "this is Marina."

Grace walked over and was so overcome with emotion when she saw this beautiful woman; she was otherworldly, of that there was no doubt.

Marina held out her hand and said, "it is lovely to meet you Grace we have heard so much about you."

"And I you, I feel as though I am dreaming, welcome to our lighthouse retreat."

They all looked at the door in unison as the most beautiful man Grace had ever seen walked in. Or did he glide?

He looked at them all with the most beautiful smile on his face. Grace looked at Matthew and he was staring in awe at the lovely man walking toward him, he felt so overwhelmed.

"Greetings brother, I am Elarquin Shothnae, good to make your acquaintance."

Matthew shook Elarquin's hand and just stared speechless, so much love, so much connection.

It was an instant knowing. "We are soul family," said Matthew. "Yes, yes," said Elarquin, "indeed we are and we have much catching up to do."

They all started laughing as they saw Grace staring at Elarquin totally gobsmacked, no words would come out of her mouth. This was no ordinary man. Elarquin's every word was like a melody, he was at least seven foot tall, with white golden hair to his shoulders and eyes of emerald green. When Grace looked into his eyes she could see the ocean, the whales, the dolphins, crystal castles, she was mesmerised. She felt mortified when she realised the others were laughing at her but she could not take her eyes off him.

Elarquin embraced Grace and she felt like she was home. He had an energy that wrapped you up and made you feel as if you would always be safe.

"I love you too Grace," said Elarquin looking into Grace's eyes. Together they travelled to infinity and back in the blink of an eye.

Grace pulled herself away from Elarquin and started laughing. "Oh my, I don't know if I can take anymore of this."

They all laughed together feeling and knowing that they had been re-united once again on this planet at a crucial time of transformation. Everybody knew that this was the divine plan and they would all do their parts.

They talked for a while, drinking coffee and eating muffins there was no feeling at all of being strangers, they were just remembering each other.

Matthew offered to take Marina and Elarquin to their room, they accepted graciously they were just starting to realise how tired they were.

Matthew felt so comfortable with Elarquin that he told him everything about himself. About being Sorin and coming from the higher dimension to be with Grace so they could help the planet and the human race with the transition that it was going through.

None of it surprised Elarquin, as he and Marina had their own story that made Grace and Sorin's look easy.

The six of them were together now and that was all that mattered.

He went back to the café to find Salome, Damon and Grace standing at the window looking at the ocean in silence.

He walked over to Grace and held her hand, they all stood now and looked, words had no place in such a meaningful reunion.

They absorbed each others energy and became one.

Damon said, "it is time we take our leave too, we have been traveling for days." Although they were excited they could feel exhaustion from the past two months' journey taking a hold of them.

There was so much to absorb. Re-connecting with their beloved friends had brought up so much emotion for them all.

They all said goodnight and went to their rooms.

Grace and Matthew could not stop talking about Elarqiun, he had such a powerful majestic presence about him.

Grace filled Matthew in on all she knew about him. She did recall that he had been locked in a different dimension in the ocean at the end of Atlantis, and it was Marina's love for him that had somehow set him free so they could be together.

She also told him that Marina and Elarquin both had the ability to morph into mermaid and merman, as was their original form on the planet when it was mainly ocean many aeons ago. Matthew somehow felt that he had heard it all before, he knew it all in his heart. All he could feel was gratitude for having the six of them together, but he knew there were two missing. Grace then told Matthew about Alanika, for she was the one that had brought them all together.

She was now in Scotland with Owen her twin flame. Matthew could feel something gnawing on the edge of his awareness something that the eight of them were here to do together.

Grace said she could feel it too, and they would discuss it with the others in the morning when they were all fresh after a good night's sleep.

Grace went to sleep with a smile on her face and a heart full of love, never in her wildest dreams could she have anticipated the events that were unfolding... a peaceful sleep came easily.

CHAPTER 12

They closed the Guest House for a month. They knew the time they had with their friends was more important than anything else. They were all having one-on-one time with each other, getting re-acquainted, they were having the most amazing time. Elarquin's and Marina's love was a force to behold.

They were both so passionate about the earth and the oceans, and they talked freely about life on other planets and in higher dimensions. Their memories were waking up, and being together somehow inspired a clarity and conviction in them all to do whatever it was that they had come together for.

Elarquin fixed the steps down to the beach, so they all went down every day. The surf was quite rough compared to what Elarquin and Marina were used to on the island, but in no way did that dampen their absolute love for it.

Salome and Damon were busy getting ready for their wedding, there was only going to be the six of them, but still they wanted it to be perfect.

There was a lovely celebrant named Marla from a nearby town, she was very spiritual, so she would be performing the ceremony and then they would celebrate on the lighthouse platform.

Salome and Damon would take their vowels at dusk when the veils between the dimensions were at their thinnest.

The wedding day had arrived, it was a Sunday, the sun was shining but it was quite brisk.

It was spring a fortuitous time to start their new commitment to each other.

The air was electric and they all could feel the light pulsing through every cell in their bodies.

Grace and Marina were preparing the food in the café, they were making a feast. They made canapes, vegetarian lasagne, cut up fruits. Marina made beautiful salads; her specialty. They were laughing and talking, the joy they all felt was palpable.

Elarquin and Damon were setting up the fairy lights in the lighthouse.

Salome was looking in the mirror at her reflection, she hardly recognized the contented woman she had become. She had been so restless, always searching, until she met Damon, and now she felt so blessed because she had all she could ever want. A lone tear escaped as she thought of the beautiful vibrant Alanika, the starry girl that had brought them all together, the only thing that would be missing from her special day.

How she loved Damon with all that she was, there was nothing she would not do for him.

She picked up a pen and started writing:

> I love you my love with all my heart
> From this day never shall we part
> You bring out the very best in me
> And into your essence I do see
> All that is good and right in this world
> All that is pure and strong
> With your love never shall I stray
> From the truth of my purpose on earth
> For you are my light, you are my rebirth
> Warrior man I give you my heart
> I give you all that I am
> You are the stars, the moon and the sun to me
> And it is your love, my love, that has set me free
> You and me we shall always be
> This my love is our destiny.

These words were her gift to her lovely man.

No words would suffice for the love she felt for him, the rest she would bestow on him with her body and soul, for all belonged to him.

She had chosen a simple dress, it was more of a toga really, she could have passed for an Egyptian queen.

She wore gold bands on her forearms imbedded with lapis lazuli and amethyst, these were in honour of Archangel Michael. He was always there with Damon and herself, he was their Guardian Angel whom they both loved beyond words. They had so much gratitude for the many times he had protected them both before they had found each other. This was why they had chosen the sapphire ring. It was his colour.

Damon looked in the mirror and saw a man that he was proud to have become. He could hardly believe that he was marrying the love of his life, oh, and how he loved the wild free Salome. She would always be a mystery to him, always new fields waiting to be discovered, never had he ever felt bored with her.

He had no idea that such a love would have found him, he had to pinch himself to make sure it was real.

In an hour she would be Mrs Salome Christos. His heart skipped a beat.

He wore a white pirate shirt with white cloth pants, he looked so handsome with his black wavy hair to his shoulders and big brown eyes.

They said their vows on the cliff overlooking the ocean, the wind stopped just for them and all was perfect.

Grace was so happy that her beloved friends were getting married on her very sacred ground, watching them taking their vows was a dream come true.

They both looked absolutely stunning in white, it was a sight to behold, all was mystical with the sound of the waves crashing in the back ground, and Marina and Elarquin looking as if they had both just stepped out of a fairytale.

They were all in this world but not of it, they were of the stuff that dreams were made of.

There was so much joy between them all as they were laughing and chattering walking up the stairs of the lighthouse.

The sun was almost down and the sky was swimming in mauves, pinks and pastel blues, it was completely breathtaking. Grace lit the candles and the fairy lights were on. Salome thought that nothing could be more enchanting than the setting they had. The ocean waves crashed against the shore in the background.

They sat down and all gave thanks for the blessings they had in each other and for the earth and all she gave them.

It was now dark and out of nowhere Grace could hear a humming sound. She remembered that sound.

They all looked up in unison to see a huge craft with blue lights beaming down on them. They were all speechless looking at each other, and then it stopped right beside them just hovering, and then a bridgeway appeared and opened on to the platform. The silence was deafening.

And then the most lovely woman with long blonde hair disembarked. Salome caught her breath; she felt like she would choke. It was Alanika followed by Owen.

Damon stood up and they walked toward each other communicating telepathically.

They all hugged overcome with emotion. And then Oriam and Stariam appeared and said, "Salome and Damon this is our special gift to you on this most auspicious occasion."

There was not a dry eye in that lighthouse.

"You have all come together in your commitment to each other, to the planet and the evolution of the human race."

Within the power of the divine balance of Oriam and Stariam they all rose above the emotion of the occasion into a certain clarity of what brought them all together.

Words were not necessary, they all knew now there was a higher purpose for this occasion and all were ready to do their parts.

We bid you now to step onto the ship for we have somewhere we must take you.

Oriam glided toward Grace and said, "Grace Bliss do you have the teardrop you received from Mother Earth?"

Grace nodded, put her hand into her bag and pulled out the crystal with the teardrop in it.

"I am aware that Grace has told you all what transpired in the cave with the essence of Mother Earth."

They all nodded. "We filled Alanika and Owen in on what you have been given Grace. This is a very sacred act indeed, never has Mother Earth bestowed this blessing on another.

This teardrop in the wrong hands could destroy this planet in seconds.

They all walked onto the spacecraft knowing they were on a mission of grand proportions.

Going onto the spaceship was like walking into an ethereal city, nothing appeared solid all was like liquid.

There was a huge quartz crystal in the centre. Oriam glided toward it and sent it an energy from his mind and they took off.

They were all looking at each other with a strange sense of calm certainty.

Alanika sat between Marina and Salome holding their hands. The love being generated between them could have moved mountains, thought Grace.

Oriam and Stariam walked around and touched all of their third eyes, they lit up with a golden light.

There was enough information in that one touch to last them many lifetimes. What a beautiful feeling it was.

Stariam said, "we have now arrived at our destination." They opened the hatch and Grace could see a light shining off the walls of the cave. They walked out one by one.

The beauty surrounding them was mesmerising.

There was water running down over giant crystals into small pools.

It was the most enchanting scene Grace had ever witnessed. Stariam said, "we are in a cavern deep in the Earth." Stariam asked them to stand in a circle each beside their partner.

Paulette Blomeley

They did this and they could barely contain the power that was beginning to surge through them all.

They held hands and a beautiful sound resonated out of the crystals around them; it was getting stronger and louder. They were all sweating profusely.

And then a massive rose quartz heart appeared in the middle of them all.

Oriam told Grace to walk into it with her teardrop. Matthew was beside her.

"Now the eight of you with your partners are to walk into the heart with total divine love for each other and Mother Earth. You are about to set into motion the biggest healing the feminine energy on this planet has ever experienced.

You, by being together, will restore the balance of the divine masculine and feminine energies. First the feminine, and all the pain women and the earth have experienced at the hands of greed and the total dishonour for the feminine aspect of self.

This planet is being annihilated with no concern for the essence of the planet itself.

They were all inside the rose quartz. It looked like pink water but was not wet.

Grace held out her hand with the teardrop on it as the crystal around it dissolved and the teardrop fell into the rose water-like substance.

A loud scream resonated through each one of them, like nothing they had ever heard. Every bit of pain that every woman had experienced throughout all time on earth was released in this one earth-shattering cry. The whole world shook as they linked hands in a circle again, they all felt the pain releasing through their bodies. Just as they approached the point where they could not take anymore it stopped and a beautiful sense of peace pervaded them.

At the spot where Grace dropped the teardrop a massive hole appeared and now there was pink and gold light pouring out of it like a fountain. They watched intently as they saw love spread over the planet, healing all broken hearts. The feminine aspect would no longer be abused by the masculine.

Oriam made it clear that it was not only men who abused the masculine energy. In some cases woman abused it also, considering we are all made of both divine masculine and feminine.

The face of the essence of the planet appeared and said, "thank you all for all you have done, you have set in motion a great healing for this planet, and the women and men residing on it. It is my body and it could not endure anymore suffering.

You have helped me release all pain for the love you have between you all is pure male/female divinity.

My deepest and most sincere gratitude to you all.

May you all go on to enjoy the fruits of your labour as you witness this planet morphing into an authentic reality where all, once again, have the ability to evolve in a genuine manner in harmony with Universal laws and not through destruction."

After Oriam and Stariam dropped Grace and her friends back to the lighthouse, they sat in silence for some time listening to the ocean crashing against the rocks under a twinkling starry sky.

Words were superfluous after one had been exposed to such magnanimous energies, such huge power with the ability to transform a planet. This planetary transformation would, in turn, transform the species living on it and visa-versa. Transforming the consciousness of the race transforms the energy of the planet.

They were all very excited about what was to come. They knew the planet could not have continued on the destructive path that humans had set it on, and knew the only reason they all had been sent to the planet at this time was to contribute in any way they possibly could to the transformation of the mystical cosmic planet Earth.

She had so much power and abundant resources within her that were untapped. Once humans were living in their authentic state the knowledge could be released without fear of it being used against good!

They chose to spend their final night together on the platform of the lighthouse, for there was nowhere in the world they could have been happier.

It had been three weeks since Marina and Elarquin had arrived and they had shared so many beautiful times together since then.

Their bonds of friendship were tied for eternity!

Alanika and Owen gave Salome and Damon airline tickets for a wedding present, an extended holiday to Scotland, staying with them in their majestic castle set up as an eco-friendly backpackers and group accommodation.

Grace and Matthew decided if they could find the right people to run the retreat, they would go over for a short stay.

Grace loved Scotland and was very excited at the prospect of walking the Scottish Highlands with Matthew.

And after meeting the delightful Alanika one would always want more. Grace was sure she saw little stars dancing around her, she was most certainly enchanting. Now she knew why Salome and Damon responded the way they did at the mention of her. Grace was sad that Alanika and Owen had to return with Oriam and Stariam, she really would have loved more time with them both. Now she had a wonderful reason to take a holiday ... one could only imagine what would happen in Scotland with them all together!

Printed in the United States
By Bookmasters